Susan Schmidt is an American
works as a bookseller. Her
published by Serpent's Tail in

Richmond
April 94.

Out of America

Susan Schmidt

Library of Congress Catalog Card Number: 93-84651

A CIP catalogue record for this book is available from
the British Library on request

The right of Susan Schmidt to be identified as the author
of this work has been asserted by her in accordance
with the Copyright, Designs and Patents Act, 1988

'Romanticizing Heidegger' was first published in *Slow Dancer* magazine

Copyright © 1993 by Susan Schmidt

First published in 1993 by Serpent's Tail, 4 Blackstock Mews,
London N4, and 401 West Broadway #1, New York, NY 10012

Set in 10½pt Bodoni Book by Servis Filmsetting Ltd, of Manchester
Printed in Great Britain by Cox & Wyman Ltd, of Reading, Berkshire

Contents

This book is dedicated
with love and gratitude
to Tom Schmidt

Special love and thanks to
Nancy Gage, Jonathan Tatlow
and, as always, to
Natasha and Anya

Medley for Nick and Jane

Track one

Nick puts 'Lay Lady Lay' on for the fourteenth time that evening. Maria the finch chirps in her cage next to the cymbidium orchid. The boys are asleep in their room and Carmen and Jane sit on an old sofa next to the record player. Nick has just come back from New York where he was a part of a group show at MOMA. He always has been rather egotistical but he is really full of himself now. He croons along with Dylan.

'He loves that song,' Nick's wife, Carmen, says.

'I noticed,' Jane answers in a rather Dietrich voice, inhaling her Kent. 'I *used* to.' Jane has just bought the Dylan album for Nick and Carmen and, as it turns out, it was all he'd heard when he'd been in New York, the big hit of the moment. Every time he plays it now the New York memories flow for him. Remembered glory.

The windows are open to a Houston night that breeds humidity and mosquitoes. A fan, positioned at the foot of the bed where Nick is lying, buzzes back and forth from side to side. Because of the airlessness of their back bedroom, Nick and Carmen have moved their bed into what would normally be the dining room. They've just had a welcome-home party for Nick, but everyone except Jane has gone home and she and Nick have peeled down to t-shirts and jeans. Carmen still wears a man's white shirt and black trousers. Not wanting to drive home across Houston so late at night, Jane asked earlier if she could sleep at their place. Beer cans line the tops of the speakers, the bookcase and the window sills. The Johnnie Walker bottle has about an inch left. Jane and Carmen sip their drinks as Nick lies there, thinking of New York, crooning away to himself.

'My clothes are dirty but my hands are clean,' he sings along with Dylan.

Jane and Carmen talk about the modelling business. Carmen is ex-Vogue, extraordinary bone structure, very Garbo. She is the most beautiful woman Jane has ever seen. Jane wonders though about Carmen's heart. So far, she hasn't seen any signs that Carmen has one. Carmen and Nick have three sons, so Jane assumes that Carmen has some kind of feeling in there, inside her. You can't have three children without feeling something. Jane rolls a joint, starts it around, and swigs at her scotch. When the joint gets to Nick he looks at it first.

'Wasted on me. Doesn't do a goddamn thing,' he says as he inhales. He passes it back to Jane, gets up to put the track on again and lies back down on the bed.

After a few moments during which the mixture of booze, grass, Houston humidity and late-night exhaustion ooze over each of them like a mosquito net, Nick, without looking at either of the women, sits up, adjusts the pillows behind his head and heaves a deep sigh.

'So, which one of you's gonna fuck me tonight?' he says, out of the blue. It's like a voice coming from off stage in some theatre of the absurd play.

Dead silence. Neither woman speaks. Carmen smiles. Jane's throat lumps. Maria flutters to a perch as if on cue and sits with her back to them. Nick returns to his crooning as though he's said nothing at all. Jane pretends to concentrate on one of Nick's paintings which hangs directly behind Carmen's head.

'Well, the least you could do,' he says after a few moments, 'is take off your clothes.' He peels off his t-shirt and removes his jeans. This leaves him in his jockey shorts.

Jane looks at Carmen as Carmen maintains her Mona Lisa.

Neither woman moves and Nick looks over at them. 'Ah, for god's sake! What is it with you two females? It's hotter 'an hell and I gotta be the only goddamn guy within a hundred mile radius who's lucky enough to be lyin' here with two ice cubes by my bed.'

Carmen smiles again but Jane's nervousness gets the best of her. 'I will if you will,' she says finally to Carmen, feeling like an eight-year-old taking a dare. Carmen laughs. After all, it *is* dark, Jane says to herself as a kind of excuse. Only the light in the kitchen and the candle by the record player. And it is as hot as an oven. Besides, now that she's thinking about it, she's never done anything like this before. Never, in her whole life.

Carmen lights a cigarette, inhales like a screen queen and looks at Jane.

'You don't know about my operation, do you?' she says, her voice like left-over beer.

'What operation?' Jane asks, thinking of Frankenstein.

'The mastectomy. My partial mastectomy,' Carmen answers, flat as an ironed sheet.

He rolls over on the bed towards them and grabs the pack of cigarettes from the table between the bed and the sofa, lights one and rolls on his back.

'She's just self-conscious,' he mutters, 'about taking off her clothes.' He's let the record continue past the 'Lay Lady Lay' track.

Jane sits quietly for a few moments and tries to discern any self-consciousness on Carmen's face which is currently turned in profile in darkness. As Jane thinks about what Nick has just said, she figures Carmen has the kind of personality that is so adept at putting up a front that she probably never even told anyone about it, the operation. Underneath it all, she probably needs support, Jane thinks. Maybe taking off her clothes would help Carmen get past her self-consciousness.

'It won't bother me,' she says to Carmen.

Carmen's expression doesn't change but, as she holds the

3

cigarette in her mouth, she suddenly stands and starts unbuttoning her shirt. Her shirt open, she unzips the trousers and takes them off. Jane follows her lead, taking off her jeans first, then, as soon as Carmen takes off her shirt, Jane takes off her t-shirt. They both sit down again in their panties. Carmen's operated-on right breast is in the dark. The light from the kitchen shines through so that Jane can only see Carmen's left one. They sit smoking.

'So, now, which one of you females is gonna fuck me?' he asks again a few minutes later, with more emphasis. 'I mean, here I am, a mother-fuckin' hot Texas night, the party's over, Dylan's on the turntable, two good lookin' women sitting in the nude . . . well, almost . . . and no one wants to fuck me.'

After a few seconds of silence Carmen moves to turn the record over. She has an amused, almost sinister look on her face that makes Jane think of a Bette Davis movie.

'His body means nothing to me, you see,' Carmen says, almost inaudibly, 'because, after all, I own his soul.' She returns to the sofa and sits down. Nick chuckles at her words.

Jane can't fathom what Carmen's said. People don't own souls, she thinks to herself. Unless they try to because they don't already have one. She looks at Carmen who is leaning her head back on the arm of the couch. Jane thinks that Carmen's apparent lack of interest is the most interesting thing going on.

Jane moves over to the bed. She's never done anything like this before. She wonders how often Nick has. But she always did take a dare. She moves next to him as he removes her panties and his shorts. His soul, she thinks as he enters her, pumping away. Dylan is still singin, only Johnny Cash is now with him on this cut. The fan whirs. Maria the finch is crouched asleep on one side of her cage. Jane can see Nick's self-portrait hanging over the sofa. Carmen smokes. Jane's blood feels as thin as thread.

'Passionate,' Carmen comments sardonically a few minutes later, and Jane turns her face to the other side, away from

Carmen. Jane's blood is boiling. Nick's soul is . . .

Later, she sleeps on the floor in the back room.

Track two

They are lying in bed smoking, listening to 'Appalachian Spring'. It's the place in the music that feels like a storm in the desert. It is one of those nights in Albuquerque when your skin feels like peeling and you think you can see in the dark like a bat.

Jane has driven over to visit Nick. He's house-sitting for a friend for a few weeks. He's come to New Mexico for the light, the colour. She's lived here now for three years and the light and colour have faded. They lie too quietly, side by side. Nick is suddenly still in a way she's never seen him, owl-quiet, deer-still.

'I haven't told you about Carmen, have I?' His voice is monotone. Nick and Carmen split up a few years before, about the time Jane moved to New Mexico and split up from her husband. She hasn't seen Carmen for seven or eight years. She knows they had a messy divorce.

Jane gets up, goes over to the tape deck and puts on a Bob Seger, something less dramatic, less demanding.

'She's out of it,' he says, 'I mean, she's really gone bonkers, loony tunes, crazier than shit.' Nick scratches his stomach which is bloated from too much beer and the green chilli enchiladas they had for dinner earlier.

Jane can't imagine what Carmen's kind of crazy would be like. All those years of knowing her and Jane still can't remember anything but the beautiful face, the elegant body, the eyes that never lit, the cold.

'A couple of months after I moved out I started hearing from the boys that she was acting paranoid. She kept all the windows shut tight all the time for fear that something, some Martian

5

creature or axe murderer might get in. Started refusing to eat certain foods because she said the government was trying to poison the people.' He lit a Benson and Hedges. He'd upgraded from Kents.

'Then one night I get this phone call, then another one, from two different people who're over there at her place. They're saying she's freaked out, that they don't know what to do. So, finally, I go over there and she's in a corner scratching at her face, and everybody's standing around trying to figure out what to do. She's talking non-stop like somebody on speed or something, only none of it makes any sense. She's scratching her face and body, staring at the television. I mean, no one knew *what* to do. Nothing I did or said seemed to help. So, finally I had to . . .' His voice gets thick and Jane watches his mouth draw tight, his eyes harden. He clears his throat. 'I had to take her to the psycho ward.'

Nick gets up, goes into the kitchen and comes back with two more beers.

'She stayed in there for a few weeks,' he continues, 'then they let her out. Then she went back in again another time, then out again. Now she's going to some shrink and I guess she's supposed to be better.' He humphs a bitter sort of chuckle and shakes his head. 'She blames it all on me of course.'

He's quiet again for a few minutes but she can tell he's still thinking about it.

'Blames it all on me,' he lets out another ironic chortle. 'Everything. I mean, she spends her whole goddamn life being fucked up and not dealing with things and pretending everything's just fine and then she cracks up and turns around and blames everything on me.' He takes another long swig from his beer. Bob Seger is wailing away.

'I went to this counselor about it one time. I was feeling so guilty it was just unbearable. He said I had to learn not to take responsibility for it, not feel guilty,' he pauses to reflect. 'But it's hard. Damn hard. The hardest thing I ever did in my whole goddamn life was to take her to that place. See her in that straitjacket.' His eyes are moist like a painting he'd never allow himself to paint.

They sit on the bed, looking out at the billions of stars seen from a mile high on the earth. Jane thinks of things she feels guilty about. She thinks of Carmen looking beautiful in a straitjacket. She thinks of Nick's success in the art world. She thinks of what the years have dragged in like a cat. Seger's voice taps at their brains as they listen to the crazy silence beyond:

'I wish I didn't know now what I didn't know then,' he sings.

Track three

'She looks horrible. I mean, you wouldn't believe how horrible she looks,' he says, sipping at his Michelob Light. He hands her an empty beer can for her to use as an ashtray. He's quit.

'I know. That's what you told me the last time I saw you,' she says. It has been a few years since they've seen each other this time.

Nick is spread out on the bed in his camper. He is visiting Albuquerque again, only this time he's brought his camper trailer with him and he has it parked on an empty lot behind his friend's house. It's a cold January Albuquerque night and inside he has the oven on, the oven door open, and two burners on his stove-top on full. His bulk almost fills up the whole surface of the bed. Jane sits in his one chair next to the oven. A TV and video machine in the corner of the camper are on with the sound turned down.

Jane is trying to visualize Carmen looking horrible. She recalls the pictures she's seen of Garbo as an old lady, those cheekbones still prominent, that remarkable mouth, those amazing eyes. Carmen couldn't look that bad, Jane concludes; she is just getting older. Fifty now, fifty-one? She wonders if Carmen's eyes ever lit.

It is Nick who looks bad. His face is as red as New Mexican mesa sand. His eyes are beginning to droop at the bottoms. The one vice he still allows himself, his drinking, has swollen his belly into a dangerous pregnancy.

He turns up the sound of the video tape. It's the film of Gauguin's life. Donald Sutherland, whose eyes look too much like Nick's, is playing Gauguin. His nose, modified for the film to look like the painter's, resembles the straight, sharp nose Nick also has. The film deals with Gauguin's last stay in Paris where he finally succumbed to financial devastation before returning to Tahiti.

'Don't know whether I should be watching this,' Nick says, his eyes glued to the set. Nick has hit a long, dry period financially. The oil boom in Houston in the seventies that fuelled the lucrative sales of his art, has bust. Houston is the desert now, as far as selling art goes. Albuquerque is just another desert, the one he's pulled his trailer to, to hang out in until something breaks for him.

The movie finishes, Sutherland/Gauguin sadly gets it together to return to the island.

'So what eventually happened to him in Tahiti?' she asks as Nick turns the theme music down and they watch the credits.

'Died of syphilis at 54,' he says. 'I've outlived him by a year. Hell, I'll probably come down with AIDS or something any day now,' he says, smiling his ironic smile.

They talk about his painting, how a gallery in New York is sniffing him out again. They talk about his sons. They talk about how he had a daughter once by a black woman. They talk about her ex-husband, his Polish girlfriend back in Houston. He opens another Michelob Light and scratches at his belly some more. She remembers his scratching his belly on and off for twenty years. He talks brave, trying to convince himself he'll survive.

She talks soft, not sure. She gives him a hug as she steps out into the high desert night, the lights from the all-night supermarket across the street shining brighter than the desert constellations. She tells him it will all be OK.

'Oh, hell, sure it will,' he says, waving away her inference.

She gets in her car and starts driving home. She thinks about his soul, about whether or not Carmen's eyes ever lit, whether Maria the bird flew away. She turns on the radio, switches from channel to channel, FM to AM, turns it off. She wonders what tape she can put on, rummages through her collection as she drives. She pulls over to one side of the dark street and stops. Turns off the motor. She looks up at the stars, brighter now, infinite.

They don't write music about this, she thinks to herself. No one ever writes music about this.

Macho

'That year, his studio burned down. His parents both died within six months of each other. His wife went mad, said spiders were coming out of the television to attack her. And his oldest son got killed getting out of his truck to help a woman whose car stalled on a freeway in a hurricane. And that was only one year. Another year he traded one of his paintings for a black Cadillac, traded another one for a round trip ticket to Barcelona to see the Gaudís. Then, another time, he had a one-man show which filled both floors of the Houston Contemporary Arts Museum, and he had it catered. Terry Allen and his band played and the museum served Lone Star beer and fried oysters. His mad, not-quite-final-ex-wife found out about the success he was having and tried to get half of all of his paintings. So he moved to Galveston, found an old warehouse, hid out, and stored his work there until the divorce became final.' Jane lazed on the couch, contentedly rapt in memories of her old lover.

'So, were you in love with him?' the man she lived with asked.

She looked around the room as if something, some object might give her that answer. 'Well, let's just say that he's one of the largest people I know. In body and in spirit,' she finally said, knowing she hadn't really answered his question.

'I asked you whether you were in love with him, not how big he is,' he said indignantly.

'Oh, I don't know. I guess you could say I was in love with his

11

. . . style. But really, if you want to know the truth, I think that one of the smarter things I ever did in my life was not to fall in love with *him*.' She lit another cigarette and stretched out on the couch as he stirred the fire. She couldn't see his face, but knew she wouldn't like what she'd see if she could.

'As though you could exercise a conscious will over such things,' he mumbled, his back still turned away from her in what seemed to be an intentionally defiant stance.

'Sometimes in a situation where the persona is that big you *can* say to yourself "no", definitely "no". You can read a man like that a mile off when it comes to falling in love. It's not always readable in every man, that's the problem,' she said to his back.

He wasn't answering at this point. She couldn't tell if he'd taken the last comment as a slur upon himself or not. For that matter, she couldn't tell if she'd meant it to be.

'Anyway,' she continued, trying to change the subject. 'You'd think I was a twenty-six-year-old starlet who'd just finished some film with Jack Nicholson or Richard Gere or one of those young guys I don't even know the names of anymore, the way you keep asking questions. It's like being interviewed by Rolling Stone or maybe the magazine section of some Sunday newspaper.' She had another sip of her camomile tea and made a face. 'This stuff is gross.'

'You love it,' he responded, tucking his legs under him as he sat down at the end of the couch as far away from her as he could get. 'The questions I mean.'

She smiled guiltily. 'I do,' she admitted. 'Telling stories of your life is the fun part when you're really getting to know someone, don't you think? It's like filling in a foreigner on your culture.'

He looked away from her, at the fire. His jaw was set in a way that made her know that he was determined to confront her on some issue or another.

'So why did you sleep with him the week before I moved in?' he said finally, very seriously, looking back at her, 'if you weren't in love with him?' He had the look on his face of a very competitive man who hadn't won a contest.

'Oh, come on, you're not gonna actually make a statement about having to be in love with someone in order to sleep with them are you?' He didn't respond. She knew this wasn't the issue he wanted to deal with right now. 'Besides, I told you about it before you moved in.' She got up and stood in front of the fire to get a little warmer and avoid having to look in his face. She didn't like returning to this topic since she had thought it was finished business between them by now. 'He was very sad,' she repeated patiently. They had been through all this before. 'He was feeling desperate. A lot of things had happened and he needed to be close to an old friend. And, anyway, I knew it'd be the last time.' She turned around to look at him and decided to add one last thing. 'I wouldn't have done it if you'd already moved in.'

She could almost see him humph as he stretched his legs out and turned his face in a profile to her.

'You don't sleep with someone just because he feels sad either.' He was not giving up. He looked back at her and she looked down. No, you didn't, she admitted to herself. She never had with anyone else before.

'You don't understand,' she said as she sat down in the rocking chair next to the fire. 'I told you before. I've known him forever and the sexual side of it hasn't mattered to me for years. Since I was very young.'

In a flash she remembered Dylan's 'Lay Lady Lay', the Nashville Skyline album she'd given him in 1969. Nick had played it over and over as he lay on his bed. She had been sitting on the sofa next to his then-wife, Carmen, listening to her claim she didn't care who he slept with because it was his soul she wanted and she already had that. Nick had put the record on again and again. Eventually he had taken off his clothes. Eventually he had asked them which one was going to come over and fuck him. Carmen told *her* to do it; that *she* could have him

13

anytime. And eventually, she had gone over to him and done it. Now, all she could remember was looking over at Carmen as he pumped away.

'Then why do you sleep with him, if it doesn't matter to you?' His voice broke her out of her memories. She looked at him and he suddenly seemed mean to her, like a sadistic judge who had just arrived at some kind of a verdict but was prolonging revealing the sentence.

'It's just old-time shit,' she finally answered, not being able to come up with any kind of an explanation that she thought he would really listen to. 'Don't you know about these things? Women have done it for centuries − let men sleep with them because they feel sorry for them or because they know it means a lot to the guy or because it's easier than putting up a fight. Besides,' she paused, not knowing how to continue, 'he says it is the only way he has of giving his love to a woman.'

'So what does he do to give his love to a man?' he retorted, seeming to grow even angrier.

'He thinks men just simply understand him. That he doesn't have to do anything with men.' She smiled a little thinking of Nick. 'It's hard to explain if you don't know anyone from that era. He's just an ol' macho fifties person who doesn't translate.'

He got up and went out the door. She could hear him outside rustling around for five or ten minutes. Because it was dark outside she couldn't see what he was doing. Because it was cold she didn't go out herself. She sat in her wicker rocking chair just rocking away, trying to figure out what else she could say or do. Something that would put him at peace, get his mind off the subject. Finally, he came in laden with armfuls of juniper which he'd apparently clipped from the two large trees at the front of the house. He was aware that she was watching him as he arranged branches on the mantel, placed more in various positions around the room, on tables, stuck in the corners of picture frames. He knelt down in front of the fireplace with the remaining branches. He closed his eyes. After a few minutes he

14

rose and went into another room, came back with a Tarot card, and placed it among the branches on the mantelpiece. Then he lit a branch and went all over the house waving it. A thick incense smell filled the house.

'Why are you doing that?' she finally worked up the nerve to ask. She hated to give him the satisfaction. He was always pulling some kind of stunt, some kind of hocusey-pocusey thing.

'To exorcise spirits,' he answered without looking at her. 'There are spirits in this house that I don't much care for.'

She couldn't grasp his sudden impulse towards the occult or whatever it was he was doing. She couldn't bring herself even to try to get into this mood of his, and she had to fight not to show how amused she was by it all. He ignored her and continued to wave some of the juniper branches and light others. He began to hum a very odd song. Softly, almost under his breath. Then he closed his eyes and stood absolutely still.

She could see he was posing, although she also knew that he believed in all of this sort of thing. God, didn't they all believe in something or another that was weird. In the last analysis, he was just an ol' macho seventies person who didn't translate, she thought, almost laughing out loud, lighting another cigarette, rocking away.

Out of America

Joanie piled her suitcases into the vw van with the Porsche engine, filled her thermos with coffee, stabilized the box full of cassettes in the passenger's seat next to her, checked the tyres and the oil, cleaned the windscreen and hit the Interstate by 7.15. She'd had the tank filled with gas the night before, cleaned the house, and left instructions on the kitchen table for her friend, Fran, about feeding the cats, dog, finches, chickens and ducks.

Now, finally, she was on the road and, with any luck, she'd be in Amarillo by 11.30, grab a sandwich at some truckstop, find a good fast semi, and flow with its slip stream all the way into Oklahoma City. Then, she'd exit on North Sheridan, head all the way up to 40th Street, park the vw in front of James' house, and run to the front door where he'd answer her with waiting and open arms.

It was a warm early spring. There had been a lot of rain recently and the high desert past the Sandia Mountains stretched green and sweet, blooming its sage, chamisa and wildflowers all along the side of the highway. Crows fluttered overhead, the occasional chicken hawk swooped down and once something — some kind of eagle she thought — heralded majestically in the distance. James loved all those kinds of things. They shared a common love for the wildness of nature, for things untouched by the devices of man, for life that flowed

17

freely beyond the fenceposts and other confines of convention. Ah, James. Unfortunately, as luck would have it, he'd had to move to Oklahoma City because of his job. Their plan was for him to transfer back to Albuquerque as soon as he could. But he'd be in Oklahoma a couple of years at least. So in the meantime they were reduced to being a commuting relationship.

She passed through Tucumcari and remembered how Route 66 used to make this little town seem so much bigger. Years had passed since she'd first travelled it, and Route 66 had now been absorbed by the wider Interstate. But the town had changed very little really – a new Holiday Inn maybe, not much more than that. She recalled that recently, the town had been stirred up for a while when two bodies had been found in shallow graves behind the old deserted railway depot. Local people got up in arms when one of their citizenry said he thought the killer might be one of those satanic cult murderers like they had out in California. But eventually the culprit had been caught, a twenty-eight-year-old man, born and raised in Tucumcari, who had simply gone 'off the track', killing the two hippies who'd been hitchhiking. He'd said he'd been drunk, and that God had told him He didn't like their looks. The man was currently on death row in the State Pen in Santa Fé. And by now, the murmurings and fears of the local people had died down and things were pretty much back to normal. People, the same people only a bit older, got up, turned on the Farm report, ate breakfast. All the teenage boys went back to wanting to become diesel truck mechanics when they finished high school, and all the girls went back to wanting to become diesel truck mechanics' wives. Not an original thought in their heads, she mused. Returning to living their days full of non-events, perfectly happy to be hanging out and back in this dusty, falling-down wide spot in the road. America was full of dusty wide spots in the roads. America *was* a dusty wide spot in the road, she grumbled to herself in disgust. But, after all was said and done, *she* was an

American too; where else could she go, what else could she be? She pressed down on the accelerator; she couldn't get out of America maybe, but she could get out of Tucumcari.

An hour later she passed the crazy Cadillacs outside Amarillo. Some artist . . . she couldn't remember his name . . . had inherited a lot of oil money and miles and miles of ranch land. So, he'd bought ten Cadillacs and had them 'planted', nose-end down, like totem poles or unexploded missiles, all in a row alongside the Interstate highway. A large water tank with 'The City of Amarillo' printed on it stood in the background. Cows grazed all around. People pulled off the side of the highway just to stare at those Cadillacs. Good stuff. That artist, whoever he was, was one who knew how to make it out of America. In every sense of the phrase, literally and metaphorically. For one thing, he lived in New York, which was not America in her view. For another, he'd made this art out of the images of America: Cadillacs, cow fields, water tanks.

She and James had often talked about how the real artist could live anywhere, work with what was around him. All he/she needed was a concept. A sense of poetry. But Joanie was not an artist; the concepts escaped her and she often found herself bogged down by the mediocrity that surrounded her. All the middle-class values that prevailed and the ever-present Bible Belt mentality, the masses controlled like sheep by the government; these things often got to her. When she was young she used to imagine what it would be like to be taken over by the Russians. Under siege. When she thought about it now it was like her whole life, here in America, had been taken over by people just as bad as any Russian; her whole life had been lived under siege.

In Amarillo she pulled into a Stuckey's truckstop to grab a bite to eat and refuel. She filled the vw first, parked it, then went inside the café part of the building. Tourist trinkets lined the shelves: paste turquoise, beaded belts – machine produced and made in Japan to look like real Native American beadwork –

polished redwood burls with seed packets, presumably redwood seeds. She bought a tunafish sandwich and a cup of coffee, and sat down in a booth. A teenage boy in a Stetson hat, obviously a local regular, was hanging around the counter, talking with the waitress as she turned the hamburgers on the grill, apparently the order for the older couple who sat in a nearby booth. She heard the boy telling the waitress about how drunk he'd gotten the night before. Then she saw the old man in the booth look over at the boy who was talking, and look back at his wife in disgust, grumbling something Joanie couldn't quite hear. Another couple and a little girl came in. The man wore a baseball cap with 'Leon Valley Tractors' written on it, and the woman wore a 'Born in the U.S.A.' t-shirt with a picture of Bruce Springsteen on the back. The little girl kept wandering over to the tourist souvenir shelves and bringing back one thing or another that she whined for her father to buy her. Joanie gobbled down her sandwich and almost scalded the roof of her mouth with the hot coffee as she picked up the bill and hurried to the counter to pay, anxious to get out of there as soon as possible.

She finally pulled back out onto the road and, just as she had hoped, she found herself behind a semi. She knew if she simply tailed the guy, he'd know where all the speed traps would be because he'd have his CB radio on. Then, once on the other side of Amarillo, he'd take off, jack it up to ninety, and she'd be in for a free ride. Of course there was a chance he'd turn south towards Dallas, but, if she was lucky...

She was. At the highway junction he headed north, shifted into a higher gear and started to pull out the stops. She slammed Copland's 'Appalachian Spring' into the tape deck and smiled at the good time she was making so far. Six hours. Another three and one-half to Oke City. Another four to James. Another four and a half to James' bed. She kept telling herself that the dark clouds building up ahead of her were being made darker by the sun shining on them ... her mother had always pointed out things like that to her . . . but after about a half hour behind the truck, large drops started pounding the windscreen, and streaks of lightning ripped across the sky. The semi kept going, but her nerve did not. She slowed down to the legal limit. The vw liked pretending it was a ship in such storms, and blew all over the place, and she knew she wouldn't have much control over it under these conditions. Damn, she swore to herself. Damn. This'll cost me a half hour at least.

The storm continued but slackened a bit just as she crossed the Oklahoma/Texas stateline. She tried to see if she could get any Oklahoma City radio stations yet, but she couldn't, so she put in the old Fleetwood Mac tape. Good driving music even though she'd grown tired of it. The rain was growing lighter but no more semis seemed to be around. A half hour later, when she got to a little town with a Texaco station, she pulled in. She asked the attendant to check the air in the tyres, and while he was doing this, she used the bathroom, and bought a coke. By the time she'd returned to the car, the attendant, a middle-aged man with bad skin like too much grease and dirt had entered its pores over the years, tried to tell her that her two front tyres were bald. He said he had some good retreads right in the garage. She somehow managed to make him take no for an answer, and pulled back out on the road. It'd only been seven and one-half hours, but she'd pushed the car and herself hard, and the adrenalin had worked overtime. She was feeling exhausted and worn down by the day. She knew that the next couple of hours would be the hardest, and she wished she could find another semi, something to concentrate on to keep her awake.

Just outside Enid, Oklahoma she saw an old lady standing beside the road, trying to hitch a ride. She was a spindly old thing, and she stood next to a cardboard suitcase, holding her handbag in one hand and an RC Cola bottle in the other. She wore a navy blue sweater over a dress that looked like something Hollywood would think a farmer's wife might wear, and a brown hat on her head that looked like a Salvation Army reject. Okie, Joanie thought, a real Okie. For the second time in her whole life she instantly thought – why not give this person a ride? The only other time she'd given a ride to anyone had been when she was coming across the Mojave one summer from L.A., headed towards Flagstaff. She'd picked up a hippy couple who were on their way to a commune in Louisiana and who had possessed between them the vocabulary of a Trappist monk. At least this old lady might wake her up, she thought. She pulled over to the shoulder of the road and saw, in the rear-view mirror, the old lady running towards her. She reached over to remove the box of tapes from the seat and open the door on the passenger's side.

'Quick, quick, speed on outa here,' the old lady yelled at her. 'Go on, quick now, hurry up 'fore they catch up with me.'

Joanie sat frozen at the wheel, taken aback by the old lady who was trembling with what seemed to be an hysterical fear.

'Well, come on, miss, quick. They're comin'! Quick, 'fore they get here!'

'Who?' Joanie said, cautiously moving her hand to the gear shift, not knowing what to do now.

'Never mind that, never mind! Raymond!' she yelled out looking over her shoulder behind her.

Joanie, again, looked into her rear-view mirror and, sure enough, she saw an old Chevrolet, hauling an Air-flow camper trailer behind it, pull off the road onto the shoulder behind her. Oh god, she thought . . . oh no! The woman was screaming at her to move, to drive. An old man got out of the passenger's side of the Chevy, and a younger one out of the driver's side. They started walking towards the vw.

'They're gonna kill me, girl!' the old lady was screaming. 'Already tried! I just climbed out the winder or they woulda. You hear me? They wanna *kill* me!' The old lady turned back from her window to scream at Joanie then looked over her shoulder again, then out the window on her side, then back to Joanie again. Before Joanie could make up her mind what to do, the old man was at the old lady's side of the vw.

'Now come on, Ellen,' she heard him say.

The old lady was screaming, 'You dawg! You big ugly dawg!' and the younger man came up behind the older one.

'Mother,' Joanie heard him say, 'Now quit all this nonsense, you hear? Let's just go, Mama.' They opened the door on the old lady's side.

With one strong swoop Ellen came down on the old man's head with her RC Cola bottle, gashing a cut above his left eye, then she continued pounding him with the bottle until her son grabbed her wrist, and the old man managed to grab the other one, and they started pulling at her, trying to get her out of the vw van.

'Wait a minute,' Joanie heard herself yelling. 'What's going on here? What is all this?' The men were too busy wrestling the old lady out of the car to answer but Joanie repeated herself. 'What the hell's going on here!' she yelled.

'I'm afraid Mama's gone off,' the younger man quickly mimed circles at the temples of his head to indicate the old lady was crazy. He put his arms around her from behind as the old man wiped his handkerchief at the open cut.

'She's been at the institution just lately, but 'scaped and we been lookin' for her all day,' the younger man said, out of breath with trying to contain her.

'I ain't!' screamed the old lady. 'Liars. They is liars. They's the crazy uns. They's mean! They wanna kill me!' The old man bent over to pick up the RC Cola bottle which the old lady had dropped in her struggle. Joanie wondered if he was going to try to turn the bottle in to get the two cents deposit.

'Got an all-points bulletin out on her. Police been lookin' all over,' the old man said, not looking Joanie in the eye. He got the old lady's handbag from the vw. They continued to wrestle with her, dragging her back towards the Chevy.

'They want my money!' the old lady screamed. 'My Daddy's money he left me. They wanna kill me so's . . .' the old lady's voice faded further away as they pulled her to the car and managed to push her inside.

Joanie sat there a second or two longer, then threw the cardboard suitcase out the passenger's side, slammed the door, locked it, locked her own, shifted into first, and burned rubber as she flew back out onto the highway. She didn't need a fast truck now. She'd push that Porsche engine to its limit all the way in. If she stayed on the Interstate she would not come across another town between here and Oklahoma City. If the Highway Patrol stopped her she could tell them she was hoping they would, then tell them why. She got the vw up to eighty, then eighty-five, ninety. No cops. There were never any cops when you needed them. Did she need them? She wasn't even sure what had happened.

She kept it at ninety, passing everything she came across. An hour to Oklahoma City. An hour and a half to James, to where someone was sane. To freedom. She was leaving the scene, escaping. She was headed towards something. Away from them. Away from all of it. Out of America. She was leaving America behind.

The sermon

'Goin' to El Rito, that be any good for ya?' the man in the wrecker tow-truck hollered at Loretta who was standing on the side of the road. One more hour of light she guessed, and snow coming maybe, and she'd already been walking and trying to thumb a ride since three, hoping for a Chrysler Imperial to come along and take her all the way to Santa Fé. Then she'd hop the Trailways bus on down to Duke City. But, hell, there hadn't even been an old Ford, much less an Imperial, and she'd forgotten her gloves. She had her suede and sheepskin lined coat on though, her present from Nance last Christmas. She looked at her hands, then quickly said OK to the man in the tow-truck. With any luck, once she got to El Rito, she'd catch a ride from some Presbyterian couple in an Oldsmobile headed back to Santa Fé from Ghost Ranch after some kind of religious 'retreat'. Boy, what people made up in their minds about how to get away from it all. Canned cream corn and breaded pork chops without salt – they'd probably had that for lunch, right after the blessing where some guy said thanks for all they had and asked the Lord to help those starvin' people in Africa. Not her idea of a whopping good time.

'Pretty raw, ain't it. Looks like snow,' the man said as she pulled herself into the cab of the wrecker. The radio was on, tuned in to the station that played church sermons all day long. Some station out of West Virginia or Memphis, one of those places a long ways away where those preachers drew a million a year from the dumb-bells unfortunate enough to pick 'em up on their radio's long-range wavelengths.

'Where you headed?' the man asked. He wore a greasy, dirty, fleece-lined denim jacket and one of those hunter's caps with ear flaps. Chewed gum.

'Albuquerque,' she answered hoping he wasn't a conversationalist or nothing.

'Got a son in Albuquerque,' he said proudly. 'He's the pastor at "Our Christ the Redeemer". You ever been there?' the man slightly turned to her but kept his eyes on the road.

'Nope,' she said quickly, hoping to cut him short.

'Yeah, been a preacher for seven years now, though I don't know why he bothers with all those souls in the big city. Lord knows, His sheep in these pastures around here don't stray so far.' He smiled a holy sort of smile. She decided to keep her mouth shut, not to say what she was thinking, that sheep were among the dumbest creatures on the face of the earth, and she'd take a good dog any day.

'Takes after me I guess, my son,' the man said. 'Lord delivered me up to be His servant in 1946,' he swelled with pride. 'Been preachin' His word somewhere or another ever since.'

She thought about his tow-truck, and wondered what a preacher was doing with a wrecker like that.

'So, this truck yours?' she asked with a tone in her voice that made him understand.

'God provides, God provides,' he said. 'He gave me this wrecker business to do five days a week so's I can spread His word.'

She stayed quiet. She thought, out of all the possible rides I could'a got me, out of all those Oldsmobiles and Jeeps and Jap cars, out of all the farmers and salesmen and waitresses going in for their night shifts, I gotta get this one.

'You live in El Rito?' she said as quickly as she could think of something to ask that might get him off the God-track.

'Abiquiu,' he answered. 'Wife's folks left her the house we live in there. But we go to El Rito and Espanola to give testimony.'

No way around it, she thought, he's gotta go back to God. She decided she might have to take the offensive, though she'd always prided herself in being a non-talker.

'On my way to my daughter, Nancy's house in the South Valley in Albuquerque. My gas station was dead as Christmas ... I run a Texaco up in Chama, you see. Two kids all day, one wanting a can of oil and the other $2.00 worth of Regular,' she shook her head in exasperation but she kept going, figuring it might get his mind off God. 'Been like that for days. So I says to myself, I says, "Loretta, just close up this place and get your old hide down to Nance. Maybe catch Wednesday night Bingo." So, that's what I did, closed it all up and started out.' She'd run out of words too fast. She couldn't think of a thing to add. Dry as beans. As she looked over at the man, trying to think of something else, *anything* else to talk about, she realized that his face had grown red, his eyes big and wild like a coyote's, and that his hands were gripping the wheel like it was a tank going into war. He was suddenly taking in short gulps of air.

'God don't want no things like Bingo,' he almost whispered. It was a black cloud kind of whisper – you could hear the thunder rumbling underneath it. 'It's Bingo and things like it that's turned us all on the paths to Satan.'

Oh, Christ, she said to herself, me and my dumb mouth. Never *ever* should open it. Always causes trouble. She ground her teeth and clamped her mouth shut. She felt the Campbell's Pork and Beans she'd had for lunch turn over in her stomach. They were on the high logger's road, the short-cut over the mountain that led to El Rito. A few sprawling flakes of snow had started to fall. She knew if she asked him to let her out here she'd never get another ride. She'd be done for. No one 'cept loggers and the occasional fire-wood cutter on this road and it was too late in the day to expect any of them.

27

'Bingo and beer joints and cards and,' he paused and looked over at her, looked at her up and down, 'Women wearin' pants.' He was silent for a second while he considered what to add to the list. 'All those cuss words kids use nowadays, and dancin' and pianos and musical instruments in the House of the Lord and ...' She could tell his list was gonna probably go on for hours, all the way in to El Rito. She could just imagine what else he'd probably have on that list. She knew it all by heart, this list. She knew it from Uncle Edgar and Aunt Hope, from Irwin Holmes down at the dime store, from Enid White's twin Edna, and most of all from Foster, good ol' Foster whenever he'd sober up from a drunk and start feelin' all guilty about it. Those were in the days when Foster could still manage to do such a thing as sober up. Before he finally kicked the bucket. He'd sit there at the kitchen table, his head in his hands, his hair all greasy, smelling of cigarette smoke from the night before. 'Cigarettes, any kinda tobacco,' Foster would add, 'bankers, Roosevelt, communists ...' Later, she remembered, he'd added Castro, Vietnam War protestors, college professors, mini-skirts, hippies, TV, the radio ...'cept for the hog report and sometimes the weather ... that was necessary ... Kings and Queens, the Pope, Women's Libbers, queers ... gays they call them now ... and liquor, of course, especially liquor right after he'd been on a massive binge ... jewelry, lipstick, fingernail polish ...

'You take your sexual intercourse,' she heard the tow-trucking preacher say, 'God gave us a man and a woman to make us His little children. Ain't had no intentions of anything else but that, and now all anybody acts like is animals, nothin' better 'an animals ... ever where everybody's actin' just like sheer animals.'

Loretta flashed on all of Nance's animals. These days Nance's place looked like some kind of farm. Every time she went down to see her there was a new creature of some kind. Two dogs and three cats and two horses and two cockateels and a couple of those South American parrots and now those three chinchillas her friend left with her. All nice animals too except it was gettin' to be a little too much.

'Yeah, the world's just become like animals. Everywhere you look there's someone rapin' somebody or there's a bunch of queers talking about that AIDS stuff, or the TV's showing a woman without any clothes on. And the women all buyin' them magazines that tell 'em how they should look sexy. And all the men goin' around whistlin' and sayin' rude things to the women when they walk down the street.' He stopped talking and just kept shaking his head. She could see that his mind was skimming all the thoughts it could possibly come up with on the subject. They drove on like that in silence for another five minutes or so. Maybe he'll calm down, she thought to herself. Maybe if I could just think of something to change the subject. She looked out the window and tried to think of something. A couple of turkey vultures flew over some trees to her right, probably having sighted a dead animal down below them somewhere. The air looked thick like a person would have to work real hard to move through it. All she could think of was Nancy. And that Oldsmobile ride she'd probably missed, and how long it would take her to walk into the next town if she got out now, and whether or not she would actually freeze first.

'And we too are animals,' he finally spoke again, this time in a preacherly tone of voice. And when she looked over at him she saw that his eyes were even wilder than they had been before. At least he sure is right about one thing, she thought; he sure looks like one kind of crazy, mean animal. She realized the preacher's tow-truck was slowing down. She could see he was looking for a place to stop. Snow was coming down now, not thick but regular.

'We're just weak, poor animals. Only there's a difference, you see,' the man continued, 'God gave us the chance to be different from all those other animals 'cause he made it possible for us to find the spirit of Jesus in us and ...' The man seemed to be trying to remember what it was the spirit of Jesus was supposed to do once you found it in you. Loretta suddenly remembered Foster after he'd sobered up and repented and praised the Lord and got all holy. How he'd take hold of her hard, and make her stop whatever it was she was doing, and come with him into the bedroom. The preacher was stopping the truck for sure now. Oh god, she whispered to herself, he's gonna say that he's just an animal too. He's gonna say he's just a sinner like all God's children, weak with his animal desires. She felt her legs stiffening, her hands grow into fists inside her pockets. She squeezed her lips together and gritted her teeth. Sure enough, the truck pulled to a stop, the man shifted into neutral, and put on the brake.

'But if God wanted us to be like animals, He would a said so,' he said in a low ghost-like voice in which he emphasized each word as if to squeeze out the full meaning. She thought it seemed like he was arguing, pleading with himself. 'Animals is what is making hell on earth!' She saw that he was trembling now. Beads of sweat had formed on his face in spite of the cold. He was worked up into a real frenzy. He turned to her. His eyes looked like rockets had gone off in them. His face looked like it had frozen and broken into a thousand pieces. She flinched as he reached across behind her and took his rifle from the gun rack. Her heart was bongos, a crazy rhythm like a jungle. Her insides felt like marbles, a bunch of marbles scattering in all directions after being hit by a strong shooter.

Holding the rifle, he opened the door of the truck and heaved himself out on the ground. He stood there for a moment looking like his feet had just touched ground for the first time in his life. He looked around at where he was, then he looked at her, an expression on his face like he'd just heard some kind of angel screaming inside his brain. Calling him, telling him what to do. Like the only choice he had was to listen to what this angel's voice said. Without another word to her, he headed towards the thick woods which stood on both sides of the road.

It took her exactly nine seconds, she calculated later, to get from the passenger's seat over to the driver's seat, close the door, take off the brake and shift into first. She'd rolled the window down a bit to be able to hear if he was yelling at her or not as she shifted fast into second, managing to hit every rock on the goddamned road but steering straight ahead anyway.

All she'd heard was the one rifle shot coming from the woods and the hiss of the radio, finally out of range of the sermon.

From one act to the next

'So, Irina and I are pretty much out of it and it's five o'clock — no, closer to six I guess, and we somehow manage to get it together to remember it's time for us to get back to her mother's house. You see, her mother had said she would have supper ready for us at six but . . . you know how it is when you're tripping . . . time? . . . who thinks about time? So, here we are in a flat off Washington Street in San Francisco, suddenly panicking because we've gotta get back to Carmel where her mother lives, and it was almost six already, and we had to drive the Coast highway which is, you know, real winding and slow, so it was gonna be at least two hours before we'd be getting back to her mother's.'

Jon and I are painting the inside of my house and he's telling me this story from the sixties when he was married to Irina. Right now we are doing my living room. The sofa and chairs and desk are pulled into the centre of the room and covered with an old sheet. There is a month's accumulation of newspapers strewn across the floor. We've been at it for an hour and . . . you know how it is . . . you start talking about one thing and it progresses to another. Painting rooms is one of those things that frees you to talk easily about anything, unlike when you're sitting around having a cup of tea and staring someone smack in the face. Your brain works differently when part of it is forced into doing something physical like painting.

Anyway, this story of his came about after the phone rang and I had to wade over the gallons of paint and tons of newspapers to answer it. It was my ex-husband wanting to know if he could use my car for a few hours since his was at the shop. This led to Jon and me talking about our exes which led us to talking about when we both first hooked up with them in the sixties, in San Francisco. Jon and I call ourselves retired flower children, the sort that never quite blossomed again, as it were, after the sixties. Sometimes it feels like we're those kind of plants the garden experts tell you not to bother with once they've bloomed. To pull up and start over again with a brand new plant.

'So, we're about a half hour outside S.F. on Route 1 and we decide to pick up this hitchhiker who we see on the side of the road. Irina was always like that. She said she owed a lot of rides to people because she'd hitched so much herself. So we pick up this guy. He's a hippy too . . . long hair, beads, the whole number . . . and it doesn't take long for us to relax with him and we let him know we're tripping and he thinks that's really far out of course. But, to our absolute shock and horror, after we've been driving a while he tells us he's running from the cops. Irina and I are pretty cool about it and all but, remember, we're still high although we're definitely coming down, I mean *definitely*, and I'm driving. I think we're going really fast, but every time I look at the speedometer it says twenty – you know how it is – so, I'm in a rather paranoid state and this guy says the cops are after him. He supposedly was driving his father's Pontiac and hit a man somewhere in Reno and just kept going. He was pretty young, eighteen, nineteen, and shit scared. And he'd just kept going until his car konked out somewhere north of Sacramento. So he'd ditched it and he'd been hitching ever since. He talked like a speed-freak, but who knows, he could've been anything. I was so paranoid I imagined all sorts of things.'

I'm sitting on the floor, painting the part of the wall that's next to the floor that requires more concentration. The kind of concentration where you find you are breathing shallower as if breathing regularly will make you take bigger strokes and mess up. Jon's on a ladder doing the part where the wall meets the ceiling and you can't use a roller.

'It's getting dark. And I'm going really slow. It's that part of Route 1 where the road curves out sometimes and you feel like you could go over the edge and go down a cliff and fall into the ocean. Irina is doing most of the talking to this guy. She's telling him why she has the name Irina, that it's Russian. That her mother is Russian and teaches at the Army Language Institute in Carmel. The guy keeps saying "Wow!" He wants to know why Irina's mother lives in America, if she was ever a spy. Irina explains that her mother was a little girl during the revolution and was even related to the royal family. The guy didn't know what a White Russian was. He didn't know there had been a royal family in Russia. He didn't even know there had been a revolution. He thought that Russians had always been communists. He kept saying things like "Man, you get a real education on the road."

'I have the car's lights on by now and it seems like we've been going in circles for hours, turning the same curves, each time slowing up to about ten miles an hour, creaking around. Irina is telling the guy about how her mother and grandmother made it out of Russia to Germany and how her mother had married a German and they'd come over to the States before the war and both gotten jobs at the Institute. How her father is dead now and her mother lives in this big house in Carmel with statues and paintings from one of the Russian royal palaces. How they should be in a museum they're so valuable but how her mother just lets cobwebs grow on them, layers and layers of cobwebs. Her mother doesn't believe in disturbing the natural flow of life, is what Irina tells the guy. I chip in at this point. I tell him how the old lady, if she draws a glass of water from the tap and doesn't drink it all, puts what's left in the refrigerator to save. There's always about three half-empty glasses of water in the fridge at all times. Along with all sorts of other left-over things that, god knows, are taking their natural flow.'

I move over to the part of the room where the fireplace is, adjust some newspapers and drag over my paint and brush. Jon gets down and moves his ladder over to where I've been sitting on the floor, climbs back up, gets down again because he's forgotten to bring the paint up with him, and then goes back up again. We're getting this done really fast. Maybe we should consider this as a possible new career. We could just paint houses all day and tell stories.

'So, as I'm talking to him, I'm gesturing a little and probably driving even slower than I was before. Irina starts to feel guilty about not calling her mother to tell her we're going to be late. I remind her that we had been in no state to talk to anyone on the phone when we'd left. And then we both realize what state we really have been in, and that we've been driving in that state all this time, and we marvel at how trained our minds are. "Like cows going home to be milked at the end of the day," Irina says.

'Just about then I look in my rear-view mirror. At first I just see lights flashing and I think, wow, the drug's still at it, then I realize it's a highway patrol car and he's behind us and his light is flashing and that means he's after us! Irina and the guy see the light at about the same time. We all just totally freak. The hitchhiker says what if it's him they're after. Irina starts looking in the glove compartment to see if there are any roaches we've stashed in there, and there are, so she manages to get a few thrown out the window before I see a place to pull off the road. We sit there like criminals waiting for the cops to come over to our car.'

Jon splatters some paint on his face and gets down to get something to wipe it off. I've managed to get some paint on the bricks at the edge of the fireplace so we're both searching about looking for old rags or something to wipe up with. That's one of those things you always forget to get together when you're setting up to paint, old rags. It's only when you're dripping with paint or in the middle of a mess that you remember, 'Ah, old rags.' I sacrifice a dish towel from the kitchen.

'The highway patrolman is a real bastard. I mean, he's Central Casting's idea of a mean highway patrolman. Polansky could've used this guy in "Chinatown." Anyway, he flashes his badge and wants to see my driver's license. He's looking at the back and front seats of the car, at Irina and the guy, flashing his flashlight back and forth. He takes my license, goes to the back of the car, writes something down on this pad he has, and goes back to his buddy who's still inside the patrol car.

'Well, of course, we practically die while we're waiting. We sit there like zombies. Literally, our whole lives are flashing before our eyes. Irina is biting her lip and her eyes are glazed over. The guy in back is looking around him, left then right, and for a moment I think he's gonna make a run for it, but he doesn't. He's scared shitless though. I sit there and think, "Here you are, twenty-three years old and you are gonna spend the next five years in San Quentin because you are not only tripping on LSD but if they search the car, they'll find god knows how much shit — roaches, stems, pieces. You're in possession, kid. And not only that, but you're aiding and abetting a hit-and-run murderer by giving him a ride." By the time I finish adding it all up, the list of crimes, I've sentenced myself to at least ten years in prison and am dying of some venereal disease and consumption as well as god knows what else you get in prison. In the meantime, they're taking hours, days, years back there in the patrol car. I see them talking on their radio. They've probably called Sacramento to see if there are any records. It's only a matter of time before they come over to arrest us. The hitchhiker says, "If they check in Sacramento, I'm a goner. They must have an all-points out on me for sure by now." Irina is as white as a sheet. She closes her eyes and starts to chant to herself.'

'Oh god!' I say as I drip some more paint on the bricks, 'I'd die. I'd absolutely die. I'd have to go to the bathroom. I always have to go to the bathroom when I get scared.'

'Irina did too, she told me later. She said she thought her bladder would burst.' Jon had finished with one can of paint and was searching for something to open up another one.

'Well, finally, the cop comes back towards the car and we all hold our breaths. This is it, I think. I'm too young a person to go to jail forever. I'm a good person. I don't deserve this. Then I remember that anti-war protest rally I'd gone to in the Panhandle a couple of weeks before. People said the CIA were there, taking pictures. That the CIA had files on all of us. Add this to all the other stuff and it was for sure I was in the pen for years, centuries.

'Anyway, the cop comes back to our car and he shines his light in at me again. He shoves my license at me, steps back from the car, moves in towards me again and looks me square in the face as he's shining his light on me.

'"You got a tail light that's out, buddy. Left one," he says, then his voice gets mean-sounding. "Listen, you son-of-a-bitch," he says, "I know I could nail you to kingdom come for probably a million things," he says, "like possession for one." He looked at Irina and the hitchhiker then back at me. "But Sacramento hasn't got anything on you so I'm gonna let you go." You could tell this was painful for him, really painful. "But you better get your hippy asses outta here so fast you're a blur, a fuckin' blur. You understand? You got it?" and I nodded at him and Irina smiled her goodie-two-shoes smile at him and the hitchhiker nodded his head enthusiastically in approval of the cop's words. I started the engine and we moved out, this time a little faster, but not too fast 'cause all we really needed now was to break the speed limit. When we got to Carmel we let the guy out on the seafront then hurried to get back out on the road which led up to Irina's mother's.'

Jon has paint in his hair and when I reach to scratch my nose I find I have paint on it, right at the tip. Paint is a mysterious thing. It's got a life of its own. Like one of those diseases plants get that you can't see. It just creeps around from leaf to leaf until suddenly, one day, you see spots all over it.

'So, by now it's about nine o'clock and Irina and I are exhausted and famished but incredibly relieved. We're hurrying to get off the road before the cop might find us again. We pull up in front of her mother's house at about nine-fifteen.'

We must be getting to the big climax in Jon's story now because he's put his brush down, is off the ladder and is just standing there talking to me, all excited.

'Well, as soon as we pull into her circular driveway, Irina's mother comes racing out of the house. She's completely, I mean *totally* hysterical. Shaking like a leaf. Her face is red and wet with tears like she's been crying a long time. Her eyes are totally wild. She's screaming "Mon Dieu, Mon Dieu," and then lapsing into Russian which, of course, I can't understand a word of. It's like jibberish, like speaking in tongues. But Irina understands and, as she's hugging her mother and listening, she looks up at me every now and then as if to say, "You won't believe this." I notice the old lady keeps gesturing towards the house and I also notice that the house is completely dark, not one light is on.

'We eventually calm her down a bit and she stops crying and we try to get her to come into the house but she won't. The three of us sit down on the steps of the front door. After a few minutes,

Irina gets the old lady to take some deep breaths and I guess
she's finally calm enough to be able to talk to me in English.
During all this I've tried to imagine what could have happened. Did someone break in? Did one of her cats die? Did
she get a phone call telling her the Russians were invading?
What?

'Finally she's calm and with a really controlled way of saying
her words, slowly, one at a time, she says, "I was in the kitchen at
about eight o'clock, sitting at the kitchen table ... I couldn't
wait any longer to eat ... you were so late ... when suddenly it
hit me ... it was like a real physical punch – that you and Irina
were in trouble. You were in real trouble. God was telling me
that you needed my help."

'I looked at Irina and she looked at me out of the corner of her
eye but tried to ignore the expression on my face and keep her
attention on her mother. The old lady started to cry again, just a
little, not hysterically, as if in relief.

'"God was telling me to help you," she says. "So I took deep
breaths and started praying. That was when I sent all my good
spirits to you, to protect you, to save you." She started crying a
little harder. After the sobs subsided a bit she blew her nose and
took some more deep breaths.

'"But you see," she said, "with all my good spirits gone to
protect you, there were none left to protect me!" She was being
what seemed to be quite rational by now, if you can believe that.
She stood up and stepped back from the house and looked at it,
as if sizing it up.

'"When I opened my eyes and looked up," she said, "they
were all around me. The bad spirits had come for me. It was my
turn," she looked at me and Irina. "That is what they do
sometimes."

'Oh, come on, Mamuschka, I said. Mamuschka was my pet
name for her.

'"They would have killed me," she answered, the tone in her
voice quite firmly stating what was, to her, a fact. "There was

nothing left for me to do except fight them off until you returned and brought back the good spirits."

'I looked at Irina again but she wouldn't look at me. She knew what I would be thinking and she didn't want her mother to think she didn't understand, didn't believe what she said. Actually, I think Irina really did believe it, only she'd never admit it. I realized there was no way I could ever rationalize this stuff, that I could never try to argue her mother out of her beliefs. To be honest, I didn't even know what I believed about all this, except maybe the old lady was crazier than I thought. So finally I said, "Look, Mamuschka, we're back now. So, we must have brought the good spirits back with us too, and if the good spirits are back now, then everything's OK, right?" She looked at the house again, then back at Irina and me and her body relaxed and for a minute I thought she was going to faint. She got a smile on her face and tears started again, only they seemed like tears of relief this time.

'"You are right of course, you are absolutely right!" she finally said and Irina and I got up and we each took one of her arms and led her back into the house.'

Jon and I were through with the living room now except for the ceiling. The plan was to leave the ceilings in all the rooms until the very last, then do them all in one go.

'We turned on the lights in the entrance hall to the house. I don't know what I expected to find, but everything was normal in the hall, just as always. Mamuschka led us towards the kitchen. When we walked through the door of the kitchen, I couldn't believe it. It looked like something out of "Poltergeist". Smashed dishes were all over the floor. She had obviously made pastry earlier, and I guess the flour had been somewhere on the counter nearby when it all happened because it was now all over everything, a layer of white powder. The fridge door was open, its light on. Pots and pans littered the floor. Two of her cats sat at the threshold, refusing to come into the room. The kitchen table had a glass of milk overturned on it as well as a plate of food that looked untouched except for the layer of flour. One kitchen chair was overturned. Whatever had really happened, the old lady had waged a real war in there, no doubt about it.'

The phone rang again. It was my ex saying that he didn't need to borrow the car after all. After I hung up Jon and I got some of the newspapers and started to lay them down in the hall. We wanted to hurry up and finish the hall as soon as we could. Halls are like that. They are the most difficult rooms to paint. There are so many doors leading into them. So many corners and edges. Not much room to move about in. Too dark. Like an intermission between rooms. Something you do to get from one room to another. From one act to the next.

Pas de deux

'**D**o you think it could ever possibly get any better?' He heaved a sigh of total relaxation, basking in his aftermath of bliss. The closest he ever came to being sentimentally romantic was after they made love.

His question struck her many ways at once. She weighed all the possible answers she could give, the ones she knew he would like to hear, then discarded them all within moments.

'That's rather hard to say,' she answered finally, knowing it was a reply he would have problems with.

'What do you mean, "that's rather hard to say?"' He pulled away from her, agitated, the magic between them suddenly having evaporated. He lay flat on his back on the bed, and looked up at the scroll work at the edges of the Victorian ceiling.

'Well, it depends on so many things, don't you think?' she said, still lying on her side, looking at the cat which sat in the window. The cat always sat in the window when they made love. It sat with its back to them as if in disgust.

'Like what, for instance?' he said, becoming more incensed. He knew she was probably right, but her answer to his elated not-really-a-question had brought him back into a harsher-than-he'd-like present.

'Oh, you know, lots of things.' She turned on her back and tried to get clear what she had meant. 'Something to heighten the romance leading up to it maybe. Or, maybe weeks of celibate

separation which would make us so horny we couldn't stand it.
Or drugs.'

'Drugs?'

'Well, yeah, maybe. Who knows? Maybe a little opium, say,
might make it out of this world.'

He thought about what she'd said. 'Like, what kind of
heightened romance thing?' He decided to skip the drugs idea
for the moment.

She looked at him and thought he looked vaguely familiar,
although she wondered. Then she thought about it and realized
he was *too* familiar. She sighed.

'Oh, come on, we've been through all this before. You're just
not the romantic type. And I am. Most men aren't romantic,
remember? We decided this. Remember we've talked about all
this before?'

'Yeah, but this is different now.' His hand was playing with
the pubic hair that stretched from his navel down to his penis.
He could think better when he did this.

'It's different now. Now I wanta know,' he said. 'I wanta know
about this "heightened romantic thing".'

'Why?'

'Because,' he looked at her and saw she was smiling at his
agitation. He hated it when she thought she knew something he
didn't. She became very superior and her eyebrows arched.
'Because I'm curious, that's all.' All this made him very
defensive. Because of her superior attitude the last thing he
wanted was for her to think he might want to know so that he
would actually *do* anything about it.

She bit the inside of her mouth and looked away from him as
if she had to be very patient and indulge him. Then she started
to wiggle her foot, something she did that made *her* think better.

'OK. Well, like, for instance. What if we were in Italy.
Florence, say. Or, no. What if we had a fight and I just got up
and flew away to Florence, and got a room, and I was feeling
miserable and spending my days trying to get over the fight.

Eating lots of gelato and looking at sunsets and tiled roofs and ibex trees and Michelangelos and young Italian men in tight black trousers who hissed at me when I walked down the street. Observing young lovers trying hard not to touch each other in certain ways in public. And it's hot, and there's lots of passionate music, not just Vivaldi, coming from every doorway. All the women everywhere show cleavages – full, round breasts wherever you turn. And everything is ripe: peaches, olives, cheese. Wherever I turn I see ripeness. And you're not there. All these Adonises keep rubbing up against things – doorways, cars, bridge railings. They keep pushing their torsos up against these things and look at me. The cats in the neighborhood where I'm staying all scream at night when they mate. The breeze that comes through the window of my room at night is warm and luxuriant and smells like mimosa. I dream of you fucking me in a river with a soft sand bottom. Fish swim all around us as we're making love. Turquoise fish. Iridescent fish. Fish with pink spots. Their mouths opening as if they're kissing the air in the water. And I wake up and you're not there. I go down to the piazza and have a cappuccino and write you a postcard. I draw lips all over it. While I sit there the sun shines down hard, and I squint as I write. The sweat fills my face and drips down my neck. I unbutton the top three buttons of my blouse. I pull my hair up and fasten it with tortoiseshell combs. Strands of it fall down on my neck, emphasizing the tender nape of it. I look up and see a swallow. I look up and see two swallows circling each other, dancing into a dizziness. A pas de deux. I look up finally, once more, and, miraculously, there you stand. You are holding a gardenia. Your eyes are black pearls. Your shirt is undone. Your hair has grown a half inch. You put the gardenia behind my ear. You say nothing. You put your finger to my lips to prevent me speaking. You reach out your hands and take mine. I follow you up a winding street to the room you have let. The doorway to the pensione is painted cerulean blue and is peeling. You nod to the matron in charge and we walk up a flight of stairs to your room. There is a bed with nothing but a sheet on it. You open the louvered windows to reveal another scene of tiled rooftops. We hear horses clomping in the street. We smell bread baking. Our teeth clatter in wanting to bite into something. Little arrows have been shot into the area between my legs. You lay me down on the bed and undress me. You undress. Slowly, with your hand, you take the arrows out, the blood inside me gorging, your fingers giving it the message to heal. When you enter, each thrust makes it better and better and better. All the toxins leave my pores. My eyes tear. Our mouths become fish kissing the air of our watered flesh. Our eyes become swallows, dizzy in circling. We make cat sounds. It is mid-day. Somewhere a church bell answers our cries.'

He lies still. She lies still. He looks at her, then turns back to himself. She looks at him and smiles, knowing he didn't like the story. After a few moments she decides to break the silence.

'You want me to tell you one about what it could be like with drugs?' she says, trying to be the straw that broke the camel's back.

He looks at her again. Sits up on the side of the bed. Scratches his left shoulder with his right hand.

'Got any cheese?' he says, as he gets up, wanders into the kitchen.

Marydell raps about girls

The thing is, they's just babies. Don't know their ass from a hole in the ground. Come straight from their mamas and their daddys — if their daddys is still around that is, which most the time they ain't a course. But anyway, they get at that age where they think they wrote the whole world just 'cause they look in the mirror and see tits on their chest, and that's that.

So you see it's like they're these little birds learnin' to fly, and they do all these test runs — skitter over here and skitter over there — and the world being as it is, they either luck out and skitter over to some OK place or instead ... most of the time, they're *un*lucky and they skitter into the greedy arms of some ol' crow who sweeps 'em up, pecks on 'em a while, then kicks 'em off the branch into some big ol' ugly bush called life. Hell, what am I sayin' — I really don't know shit about birds.

I just know a hell of a lot about girls.

But now boys is a different ball game though. It's been my experience that boys get so wrapped up in where to stick it, they ain't got no time to think about who they's actually stickin' it to. You know? All the time racin' around like ants is in their pants. Alla time makin' some plan that's gonna get 'em into trouble. Some mama at home tearin' her hair out, thinkin' that boy's gonna be the death of her. Settin' out dinner for 'em at night, pretendin' they're gonna come right in that door at any moment and everything'll be just fine. Underneath imaginin' they's possibly lyin' out on some road somewhere squashed in a car wreck or somethin'. And when they do finally come in, those mamas is afraid to say anything to 'em for fear they'll run away just like their ol' man did. Shit. Those mamas should be so lucky. Good riddance's what I say.

But mamas is mamas. Can't say what daddys is. Mamas is rocks though. Real Gibraltars. Always there. Even the crazy ones, the ones you wanta kill, the ones that nag at you till you see red or make you feel sorry for 'em so you'll do what they want or get so hysterical you wanna slap 'em in the face like in the movies. Whatever. They's always there really in their hearts. You see, I figure they got something in their brains nature gave 'em that makes 'em be that way.

But anyway, like I's saying. Those babies. The girls. I seen 'em come and I seen 'em go over the years. Some blue-eyed doll with blonde hair like angel rope walkin' on the arm of some boy who calls himself a man or some man who thinks he's still a boy. Lookin' up at him like God just came down. The great protector. The answer to everyone's prayers. Or some sweet black-haired beauty with eyes the colour of spring leaves shows up with Mr Wonderful who's twice her age and read a book once. Hell, they think the sun rises outta his asshole. Like it's never gonna set. Even those spunky red-haired sweeties with freckles and eyes like too much light got in 'em go outta their way – I mean they work HARD at findin' some guy who's gonna do the best job he knows how to fuck 'em up.

It's like . . . yeah . . . it's like they make a list. They do! It's like they's got this list in the back of their blocked gummed-up brains: TEN TOP THINGS I NEED TO DO TO MAKE MYSELF COMPLETELY FUCKED UP. And then they go about trying to cross those things off that list.

These days, well, most other days for that matter I guess, people could probably accuse me of being a man-hater or something the way I go on. Well, it ain't exactly so, no. I mean, when they get older some men's pretty OK. Not great maybe, but

OK. Some of 'em learn along the way. 'Course, they's mainly been taught by women. And a course, if they're any good at all, they, the men, get all the credit. Shit, they get credit for being anything worth even a hill a beans. But, hell, I guess that's just the world.

But it's the girls I'm talkin' bout. The girls with their clean sheets of paper for faces. Such shiny stars. Such twinkles. They got their polished nails and their bag full of drug-store make-up and their lolly-pop lips and their spider-leg eyelashes and they hit town like the movies have been waiting just for them. Lookin' for the director. Lookin' for those spotlights. I just wanta wrap 'em up in a blanket, set 'em down in my lap, push back that ratted hair, and rock 'em to sleep. I wanta tell them, 'Honey, you're the gold in the mountains. *You're* the sun that never sets. You're the moon on a hot August night that keeps the birds awake. Don't be no water in no river rushing to get downstream and get all muddied up. Don't throw your meat to those dogs.'

But would they listen? Shit! One thing I left out is their ears. Something happens to girls' ears when their tits grow is how I figure it.

Naw, they just gotta go through it like me. Like I did. Hell, I went stone deaf when I got hair down there. Could only hear a voice if it registered in the low range. Thought my mama was this crazy ol' lady who had nothin' to say and when she did, it was jibberish. Couldn't tell me nothin'. And boy, I skittered from limb to limb with the best of 'em. Got pecked so bad you woulda thought I'd be bald by thirty. Got pregnant. Had a couple of girls of my own and got pecked some more. Then I had to watch *them* fly off and get pecked too.

But in the end, I guess you could say I did OK. I mean, not great maybe, but OK. Not exactly what I thought I'd be like maybe, but OK. That water in my river runs pretty damn clear now. There ain't much gold left in my hills anymore maybe, but ever now and then there'll be a night, some hot August one more than likely, when I'll shine. I'll shine so bright ever little bird just chirps away. Ever little bird just chirps away to their heart's content.

Uncle Vanya in New Mexico

In Beth's view, Damian is the kind of man who makes you want to open your mouth and sigh ah. Or, to put it another way, he is the kind of man who makes you clench your teeth to keep you from opening your mouth and saying ah when you see him. He is lip-smacking stuff. Good to the last drop.

Beth believes these kind of men have become a rare breed. Who knows, maybe they always were. Like a flower or a dog people pay lots of money for. Only you can't buy men like him. His eyes are purple thistles against an autumn sun. You have to sit on your hands to keep from running them through his luscious hair. He is too much. An abundance. A surplus crop of a man.

And what is she? In her judgement, Beth is a little sheath of wheat that popped open too long ago to mention. She's a pale figure of a woman who always looks back at her own shadow. Her eyes are muddied shoe buttons, and her hair, even when clean, reminds her of something you'd have to put gloves on to touch. Her body's like a mongrel in a third world country that gets fed only if she catches the food herself and nothing else beats her to it first.

Side by side, she decides, you'd have to measure her and Damian with different sticks. You'd have to put on different glasses to inspect each. If they were objects, he'd be a ladder to some kind of heaven and she'd be a footstool at the rim of a bottomless pit.

The camera of her focuses in close. It sees his teeth twinkle like lost stars. It sees his nostrils flare like trumpet flowers. It sees the hairs on his arm glisten like gold dust. She watches, (through the aperture of the lens of her mind), the light dance across the surface of his eyelids. She imagines her fingers are that light and they touch a skin that is more than silk. They wander to the edges of his eyes and feel the feathers of his lashes.

'You got anything to drink?' his voice suddenly breaks into her reverie and she responds as though having been issued commandments on tablets of gold.

'Oh, of course! What would you like?' she answers, thrilled to be able to do something for him.

'Well, a beer'd be nice.' She imagines she's the liquid slipping through his lips, across his tongue, down his throat. She goes into the house and gets a Tecate, pops off the top and brings it out to him. He's now got his hands behind his head as he lies on the grass of the lawn he's just cut. It'll be the last mowing until spring. Soon, all his clients will send him Christmas cards. There'll be nothing for him to do, work-wise, so he'll begin to live off his savings like he's planned. At last he'll have plenty of time to hole up in his den like a bear and read the things that need to be read.

He takes a swig. Ah, he says as he sips. Ah. He reaches into the small backpack he's brought with him. Pulls out a paperback, opens it to the place he's put a bookmark. Starts to read.

She catches a waft of the new-mown grass and gleefully realizes she has thought of something she can say to him.

'Damian, I was wondering. Do you think we should leave the grass cuttings on the lawn or rake them up?' she asks, trying to make her voice sound friendly and not demanding.

'Leave 'em on. It'll mulch the grass and hold in the moisture.'

He's a professional, she thinks, so he must know what he's talking about. But she also thinks she remembers reading somewhere that doing this sometimes causes molds to grow. She quickly banishes the thought.

He continues reading, she notices what the book is, and grows excited again at the idea that she has something else to talk about with him. She studied Chekhov in college. All those years ago. But even though she may be a little rusty, it's something she knows about, something they may have in common.

'I see you're reading Chekhov. Did you ever read *Uncle Vanya*?' He doesn't look up and she feels like a paper doll, thin and waiting for a wind.

'Yeah. I like *Seagull* better.'

'Oh, everybody likes *The Seagull* better because they feel sorry for the girl in the end. But really, *Uncle Vanya* is so much more like life, don't you think?' When she sees that he is not going to answer, she cringes at her big mouth. She's just put forth too many disconnected ideas. She's made too large a jump in her comparisons. He looks at her, then turns back to his Chekhov, making a double chin as he cranks his neck.

Just then, the black Ford pulls into the driveway. It looks like it has had a new paint job, but she knows Joe's just finally had it washed and waxed. Eleanor gets out of the passenger's side. Eleanor used to be Beth's best friend until she met Damian. Beth doesn't see much of her anymore. At first Beth had been a little hurt that Eleanor had let herself be taken over by a man to such an extent that she never saw any of her old friends anymore. But when Beth saw the man who'd taken Eleanor over, she didn't blame her. But regardless of all that, regardless of the fact that she and Eleanor are no longer close and Eleanor now has Damian, Beth still thinks Eleanor is remarkably beautiful, beautiful to the extent that she seems almost exalted. If anyone asked Beth, she'd say that Eleanor looks like the diamonds in a crown not seen in public for a hundred years.

Joe gets out of the driver's side, comes to the front of the car and leans against its bumper. He appraises the hair-cut the lawn has just got, and folds his arms in questions. If Joe were a vehicle, Beth thinks, he'd be a '69 GMC pick-up with the springs sticking out of the upholstery on the driver's side. If he were a song, he'd be background music and no one would sing along. As for his own opinion of himself, Joe has always thought of himself as being about sixty-five years old and still not knowing what any of the questions of life really are, not to mention the answers.

Joe and Beth watch as Eleanor wafts over to Damian. Her hands move like a river swans would choose to float on. Her breathing seems to push her forward like a feather some angel would blow. She bends over him in a slow-motion arc. He strains upward and touches her chin. Their eyes lock like in a Greek tragedy before the tragedy happens.

Beth looks at Joe and Joe looks back at Beth. If they were lovers Beth and Joe would be something sour in each other's soup. But since they're not, since they're only old friends who happened to end up sharing a house together, they are like salt and pepper, condiments sitting side by side on a shelf, waiting to be added to someone else's soup. Unfortunately, to each of their dismay, the soup of Eleanor and Damian appears to be perfectly seasoned.

Joe comes over to where Beth is sitting on the steps of the front porch. His face is flecked like a wasp's nest, the skin red and pitted. His eyes are rabbits hiding. He sits down on the porch, leans his elbows on his knees and starts running his fingers through his hair.

They continue to watch as Damian rises and stands beside Eleanor. Beth thinks: They are exactly the same height no matter what stick would be used to measure. Joe and Beth sit side by side exactly the same depth.

If there had been music, Damian and Eleanor would have waltzed. Beth and Joe would have worn black.

Eleanor and Damian move over to his vw bus which is in the driveway next to where Joe has parked the black Ford. Eleanor says, 'Well, I guess we'll be on our way now. Thanks for the lift, Joe. See you soon, OK?' and she waves goodbye as though she has a handkerchief with lilies-of-the-valley embroidered at the edges. Damian waves goodbye, gets in the bus and assumes the wheel like he is setting sail across the Aegean. They back out the driveway and head off towards the hot springs where lichen grows on rocks that surround green glades of forest grass that wait to be lain upon.

Joe runs his long bony fingers through his thinning hair again. He finally stands and so does Beth. They are insects, not the long stick figures the Anasazi drew, but more like praying mantises without a prayer. They both go inside the house, into the kitchen. Joe gets the jar of brown rice down from the shelf and Beth retrieves an onion from a basket. She cries when the onion juice leaks on her knife, and stops crying as soon as she puts the frying pan on the stove, puts a little oil in it and adds the onions.

'Think I'll rake up those grass clippings,' Joe says with a sigh, adding the brown rice to a pot of cold water and putting it on another burner of the stove.

Beth remembers what Damian said about the grass but she doesn't tell Joe. The truth is, she doesn't care if the grass lives or dies. The two have their backs to each other. Beth looks out the window that opens towards the east, towards the Sangre de Christo mountains. An apple orchard, freshly picked of its fruit, awaits winter. But Beth stands there long enough to picture cherry trees seriously responding to spring. She sees herself walking through the orchard in a white dress. Then someone beautiful like Damian coming towards her to smooth out its wrinkles.

Joe looks south, sees another flock of sandhill cranes circling the Rio Grande, headed towards the Bosque del Apache. But what he imagines is mud tracks on the dirt road after melted snow, geese flying north. Irises to match Eleanor's eyes.

They both turn back to the fridge, catch each other's eye, look away. They wish they could not see what is really there. Wish it was another thing, some other time, some other place. Some other. They wish they knew Russian. Wish they knew something to say – anything – in a language that could explain.

Romanticizing Heidegger

The sandhill cranes had started their migration early this year ... the end of February ... and Jane stood in total wonder at them again. No matter how many times she'd seen them they always struck her as miraculous. They spiralled across the white jet trail and the wafts of heat clouds that suggested the possibility of changing weather. But, so far, only the pollen count had changed, having been whipped up by the dry winds. She sneezed her seven kitty sneezes, and when her nose had cleared, she sniffed at the smoke that drifted over from a back yard where someone was burning weeds.

She lay back in the lounge chair on the patio, unbuttoned one more button of the lightest-weight shirt she had brought with her to New Mexico, and thought about Heidegger. This morning she had finally made it to the El Camino Café for Huevos Rancheros and a good farewell talk with Julia. Julia was in the middle of studying Heidegger in one of her philosophy classes at the university, and Jane loved the fact that she could get filled in on the gist of him without actually having to read him herself. Thank god. She'd always loved learning about those kind of people, their bottom-line-thinking which they had become famous for. But it always seemed to make more sense, sank home for her in a deeper way, when someone else told her about it like gossip. Or if she read the ideas in a novel and the philosopher's name somehow got mentioned in the process. So she was delighted that her friends still took courses in philosophy and classical music and art history, and loved to talk about them with her.

Later in the conversation Julia had asked her what her next step was going to be now, how she felt about going back to England. What she was going to do about her marriage. It was like when everyone had asked her six weeks before how it felt to be back in New Mexico. She would sit there feeling like the pause button on the video player; her feelings stopped behind a frozen image that shook as it held in place.

So Julia had asked what next, and the pause button had been pressed, and the computer of Jane's mind had done a search for the England file. When she found it, she entered the part of the file with her husband on it. She wanted to smile and cry at the same time. She remembered past separations from him, how she had romanticized him, their relationship. So, when Julia had asked this time, she found herself explaining this, that she had been blinded by being a romantic; she was going to have to give it up. She heard herself say she was going to have to compartmentalize her romantic feelings, hang them like dresses on hangers in the closet to be taken out and worn only for certain occasions, such as for travel or going to the movies. Get down to the 'Authentic Self' as Heidegger might have put it.

What she had meant was, that her romantic needs were ruining her third marriage. What she had meant was she was returning to a person who danced around the word 'love' like it was hot coals he was being forced to walk on. What she had meant was, if he couldn't love her, she would have to deal with that fact. One way or another. And one way to deal with it was not to want it. And one way not to want it was to convince yourself it was something only a romantic needed. If you stopped being a romantic, then you wouldn't need love. Logically speaking. What was it Julia had said about Heidegger's views on pure logic?

She was confused though about his mysticism. According to

Julia, Heidegger had died a mystic. She supposed she was
wading into dangerous territory when she put layman's
Heidegger next to romanticism next to mysticism. She
imagined Julia used the word 'mystic' because it skirted the use
of the word 'soul' which, god knows, every single goddamn
philosopher in the world got short-circuited on eventually. She
tried to picture Heidegger writing poetry in the sixties, like Julia
said he had. She'd fortunately never read any; she could just
imagine what it would be like. But how had he gotten to that
point? Had something gone soft in him in his later years to make
him do such a thing? Had he felt his old synapses oozing with
something he just couldn't explain, like the feeling one gets
from good jazz when one realizes there is something there
between the notes?

As she was recalling her conversation with Julia, she began to
realize that a tree was masking the sun. She got up and
readjusted her lounge chair to catch more rays. Another group
of cranes bleeped overhead, their sounds seeming to have
something to do with propelling them in their circular ways
towards the north. She imagined their bellies to be full of grain
from down south, for them to be euphoric in their frenzy,
ecstatic with instinct. What inferior beings humans were to be
in possession of so many faculties that prevented them from
experiencing ecstasy.

She wondered if Heidegger had ever reached an ecstatic
experience. She realized she was romanticizing ecstasy. She
realized she was romanticizing Heidegger. She was romanticizing the sandhill cranes. In forty-six and one-half hours she
would be romanticizing her holiday in New Mexico. She'd even
romanticized not being a romantic.

She sneezed five more sneezes and decided she'd had enough
sun for the day. It was one thing to return to the continuing
bleak English winter with a tan, but another thing to return
burnt to a crisp, as if the rest of the world suffered a roasting that
only the British were wise enough to avoid. She returned to her

room and suitcases. So far, there were thirteen books, four cassette tapes, a video tape of 'True Stories', six dinner plates in southwestern colours, four plastic glasses with cacti on them, a bottle of tequila from Mexico, and a black satin cowboy shirt for her husband, all to be packed among the clothes she had brought over. She wondered what Heidegger used to wear as she tried on her new black thermal undershirt and pulled on over it the new turquoise sweater. She was trying to decide whether or not it was what she wanted to wear on the plane back to England. Whether she should be wearing it as she got off and her husband met her just outside customs. She imagined Heidegger wearing black turtlenecks in his later years. Or, who knows, maybe someone gave him a pink cowboy shirt and a turquoise bolo tie. Maybe he listened to rock and roll every morning when he shaved. Or maybe he simply sat in a back garden somewhere, watching birds migrate, wondering if their music made them move north. He just sat there and wondered and wondered and wondered as he counted the 367th wave of birds until, all at once, he started making their sounds, imitating their song and he got stronger and stronger, and louder and louder, and more like the birds till he stood up from where he was sitting, closed his eyes, raised his face to the sun and screamed STOP! JUST STOP! DO YOU HEAR ME? STOP!

But they didn't, and he went back inside, and he never sat in that back garden again.

Learning French

'But I want somebody now!' Vera said to Alex. 'I want a man so bad I can't staaand it.' When Vera talked this loudly in public and drew her words out in such an exaggerated way Alex always got embarrassed. The English thought Americans spoke absurdly loud as it was without having to be subjected to Vera when she was in one of her moods.

'I mean, what am I gonna do?' Vera wailed. 'My hormones are just raaaging.'

Alex smiled a sheepish but tolerant smile at Vera and tried to be supportive. 'But Vera,' she said, 'You've been doing so well lately. I mean, look, you just got back from Paris. Your first trip to Paris and you managed a fling. Not everybody can say that.'

Vera and Alex were wandering down Tottenham Court Road, trying to escape the boredom of another night at home in their flat.

'Well, I guess the good thing about the Paris thing is,' Vera said, 'it made Hans not the last one. I can really forget him now because I know there will be others. When you're in love with somebody and it ends you always think there'll never be another one.'

Alex had been relieved when Vera and Hans had broken up because Vera had obsessed about it for months until it had finally happened. But now all Vera obsessed about was wanting to have another relationship.

'But, où sont les hommes!' Vera moaned, distinctly separating each word from the next instead of flowing the words together as would a person fluent in French.

'*Mais* où sont les hommes,' Alex corrected, managing to flow the words together a little better.

'I'm getting hungry,' Vera said. 'Wanna go to our veggie Indian?'

'Sure,' said Alex, relieved to have the subject changed.

'Why is it that having had a one-night stand after months of no sex makes you feel like you've just got to have it?' Vera continued on the subject of men after all, much to Alex's dismay. They were making their way down into the underground.

'You mean food?' Alex said, knowing exactly what Vera meant, but feeling rather devilish.

'No, silly, SEX!' Vera exclaimed loudly and Alex cringed.

'Because you're stimulated, that's all,' Alex almost whispered, resigned to the fact that Vera wasn't going to shut up about it. 'Those emotions that you've suppressed all those months have been reactivated.' Alex thought that sounded right although she was just guessing. As for herself, she had repressed her own sexual feelings for so long, she wondered what she'd be like if she ever had the opportunity to have sex again. Lately she'd been fantasizing about being an old lady living alone, having been celibate for thirty years and actually content with the situation.

'Le Métro!' Vera said when they got to the platform. 'I just loved the Métro. It was so clean and spacious and bright.'

'And quiet,' Alex added, wishing Vera would be.

There was a queue when they got to the Diwana but after a relatively short wait Vera and Alex were seated at a table near the front of the restaurant. They ordered tea while they were deciding what they wanted to eat.

'La carte,' Vera said, pointing to the menu, 'Il est la carte.'

Alex raised her eyes up into her head in reaction to Vera's pronunciation.

'So how are you going to say "bhel poori" with a French accent?' Alex kidded Vera.

'Belle pouri,' Vera tried.

'How come it sounds Danish when it comes out of your mouth?' Alex said. 'Only you can pronounce Indian words with a French accent that sounds Danish.'

'It's what we women of the world tend to do,' Vera shrugged, sitting back in her chair and striking a pseudo-sophisticated pose. 'We sometimes get our languages confused. Not to mention our accents,' she paused. 'And our men . . . les hommes . . . los hombres . . .'

The restaurant was crowded and, after the waiter had taken their orders, he asked if they would mind sharing their table with two other people, a couple. Vera and Alex moved over, still facing each other. As the newly-seated couple spoke to each other quietly Vera began to describe to Alex her last night in Paris.

'I'd decided to treat myself to a good meal my last night. I'd even ordered a glass of wine, which I never do of course when I'm on my own. *He* was eating at a table across from me and it was one of those times when you've noticed someone and you know they've noticed you too. We kept establishing eye contact and eventually he came over and asked if he could join me for a glass of wine. He spoke English, thank god. And we talked a long time, then went to a bar afterwards and had a couple of drinks and, well,' Vera gestured as if to imply 'That was that.'

The couple sitting next to them pretended not to be listening, as if they were at a separate table. But, eventually, Vera and Alex realized that the couple were taking in every word they said. Much to Alex's dismay, it became obvious that Vera was enjoying this covert attention because she began to elaborate upon the Frenchman, going into every detail of his appearance, every crumb they had eaten. Then, playing it for all it was worth, she began to describe how sexually aroused they had become.

'It was only much later at the bar that the other guy came in,' Vera suddenly added this new dimension to her monologue, somehow changing her tone, looking at Alex and winking. At first Alex didn't understand what Vera meant by the wink.

'What other guy?' Alex asked, wishing she could change the subject and trying to figure out what Vera was up to.

'The other guy . . . you know . . . in our three-way,' she paused for dramatic effect and realized Alex was showing no signs of picking up on what she was doing. 'The "Ménage-à-trois" as they call it in French.' Again Vera winked at Alex, a big wink this time. Alex's mouth dropped open in disbelief as Vera motioned slightly with her head in the direction of the other couple. It took a couple of seconds but Alex finally put it together: Vera was making all of this up for the benefit of the couple sitting next to them.

'His hair was really wild, this other guy – even wilder than mine,' she fluffed at her curly salt and pepper hair. 'He'd been driving around in his red MG with the top down.' Alex deflated into her seat and sighed as she rolled her eyes up into her head. 'He was cute too, only short.'

The waiter arrived with their food and another pot of tea. They started eating and were both aware that the couple had shifted their weight and were managing to say a few polite words to each other. Alex tried to ignore Vera, hoping that the food would get her off the topic.

'This other guy did some kind of relief work in Botswana,' Vera eventually continued between bites. 'He kept saying I should come visit and that he could find me a job. And I kept saying, "Listen honey, if I ever go to Botswana I want to sit on a veranda and drink!"' With this they both laughed. Alex, in spite of herself, had to admire Vera for her imagination and sense of character. The couple were now absolutely silent. The waiter had brought their food and they were eating, but Alex and Vera noticed they had the distant looks on their faces of people absorbed in eavesdropping.

'So anyway, it was weird in bed,' Vera took it one leap further. 'At one point, we lined our heads up at the headboard and the other guy, Jean's friend, Claude ... CLAUDE! ... that was his name, can you believe it? ... anyway, ol' Claude's feet came up to my mid-calf!'

They heard the man next to Vera drop his fork on the floor. He politely apologized for having to move around and disturb Vera as he reached under the table for the fork, then ordered another one from the waiter. His face was an odd combination of being flushed and too white. His partner, sitting opposite him, put her hands in her lap and waited until another fork had arrived, seemingly unable to continue eating until he did. After things had settled down again they all ate silently for a few more moments.

'What was weird was the next morning,' Vera said, putting her napkin down on the table. 'Claude was gone when we got up so there were just Jean and me. But Jean acted bored with having to take part in any conversation. He was totally different from the night before. The night before he couldn't stop talking about all the things he wanted to show me in Paris. I mean, that morning all he wanted to do was fuck. And then when it was over he acted like he had a million things to do, none of them including me. I've heard that's the way French men are. They like the conquest. But once the conquest is over ...' she paused for dramatic effect, 'then, so is their interest. C'est la vie.'

The waiter brought the check and Alex seized the opportunity to make a move. She stood and reached for her bag. Vera rose too, following Alex's lead. But for each of them to be able to leave the table, the other couple would have to stand to let them get through. As they did this, the man knocked his fork off his plate once again. Vera picked it up as she passed by and smiled sexily, handing it to him. He was still staring at the fork as they left the restaurant.

'Damn it, Vera, why'd you have to do that?' Alex said once they got outside. She'd been amused in spite of herself but she felt resentment towards Vera for taking it for granted that she would want to become involved in such games.

'It was fuuun,' Vera said, acting hurt that Alex hadn't enjoyed the escapade.

'Well, maybe it was fun for you, but you ought to think of others before you automatically engage yourself in one of your little games. It was embarrassing, not only for them but for me.'

'Ah, come on, Alex, it was just playing. Didn't you even enjoy it one little bit?' Alex sighed in resignation as she looked at Vera out of the corner of her eye. After all, Vera was always doing things like this. And Vera was her friend. If she was going to continue to have Vera for a friend she would have to accept her as she was.

Alex gulped down her irritation and conceded. 'I guess I'm just not in the mood for that kind of thing tonight.' They continued their walking, heading towards Trafalgar Square.

'I know,' Vera said. 'You're just horny like me only you show it in different ways.'

Alex stopped abruptly on the pavement. She dropped her hands down by her sides and stared with disbelief and anger at Vera.

'Vera, now I want you to listen to me and listen good. Everything in life does not automatically come down to *that*. Just because that's what you obsess about does not mean that every other human being on the face of the earth is going around being horny.' They were both amazed at the firmness and intensity with which Alex had delivered her words.

Vera stood with a stunned look on her face for a few seconds then turned away and walked over to the kerb at the side of the walk. Alex could see that she was starting to cry. She now felt guilty and angry at the same time. She felt she'd had a right to say what she had said, but it had obviously been too much for Vera to deal with.

'I've done everything wrong,' Vera sobbed. 'It's like none of it's adding up. I mean, I've got no family. I don't even have a lover. I'm forty-five years old and too old to keep playing tourist and too young to get a thatched cottage in Dorset and raise a few sheep.' She pulled out a tissue from her pocket and blew her nose loudly.

'*You're* too old! I'm a forty-six-year-old photography student and I don't even *like* photography,' Alex said. The two women looked at each other and broke into smiles. It had always been like this with them. One inserting a needle into the bubble of pressure that built up inside the other until it got released. Smiling, always smiling after.

They reached for each other and hugged, feeling like each was the medicine they had just taken to get better.

Alex opened the door for Vera when they arrived at the St Martin-in-the-Fields crypt restaurant. They got a pot of Earl Grey and took a table at the back of the dining area. They sat silently for a few moments, drinking their tea.

A man carrying a cello case came into the crypt. He was young, in his twenties, with frizzy blond hair and wearing a tuxedo. He found a table near the door, parked his cello case there, went to the service line for coffee and returned to his table by way of Alex and Vera's table. He caught Alex's eye as he passed.

'Kind of an English Gene Wilder, don't you think?' Alex said. 'A gay English Gene Wilder,' she added as she watched him walking back to his table.

'I want a kitty,' Vera suddenly burst out, her thinking coming from nowhere Alex could discern. 'I miss kitties and doggies.' Vera was obviously changing gears, reclaiming her old spirit. 'The thing I miss most in having to live in a stupid flat in London is no animals and you hardly ever get to meet one so that you can become its godmother or something. Let's walk down to the Embankment. Maybe we can find a good stray cat to pet.'

'Stray homeless person is more like it,' Alex said, but she stood up, feeling that it might be something to do to make Vera feel better.

They made their way to the front door of the crypt. Vera stopped to check on the hours the restaurant was open. At that moment they saw the man who had been carrying the cello case look up from the newspaper that he had spread across his table. He didn't look at them but pointed his head in their direction as he stood, and started talking to them as if he'd been carrying on a conversation with them, as if they were old friends.

'How long has it been,' he said, turning towards them, 'tell me, how long has it been since you've read a really good, I mean a *really* good obituary,' he said. Vera looked at Alex. An expression of having been rescued stretched across her face. She moved over to the man's table. Alex heaved a sigh, wandered over to the table and sat down.

Vera and Alex go busking

V era was having a hard time getting the accordion into its ancient case. One of the stops was broken and stuck out permanently, so that no matter how she tried to angle it in, it wouldn't slip down into the worn velvet interior of the case. To make matters worse her wig kept going wonky. Swivelling about her head as she moved around, the fringe consistently ended up looking like someone had cut it to taper down an inch longer on one side than on the other.

Just as Vera finally managed to wedge the accordion into the case, Alex clomped into the kitchen.

'I think these red stars are gonna fall off,' she said, looking down at her shoes. She put one of her feet up on a kitchen chair, and dabbed at one of the red stars she had just glued to the freshly painted gold tap shoes. 'The red bows though,' she held a foot up to Vera, 'Now you gotta admit, they are the crowning touch.'

Vera put the accordion case down on the floor and adjusted her wig. 'You should be wearing this wig,' she said pointing to her red head. 'It would match.'

'Nah, I prefer these Heidi braids – they go with my closeted Doris Day alter-ego.' Alex pulled at the thick blonde plaits that hung down across her breasts. Tufts of her graying hair stuck out at the sides of the wig at her temples.

They gathered up their things. Vera threw her backpack over

her shoulder, and picked up the accordion case. Alex tried stuffing her arms into her jean jacket and finally gave up.

'No way,' she shook her head. 'These peasant blouses weren't designed to fit inside Levi jackets.' She tapped her way back down the hall to her room to retrieve her bulky down vest instead. She grabbed her Sainsbury's bag that clattered with its contents. 'Damn castanets,' she swore as she found a sock and stuffed the castanets into it to keep them from rattling about.

'Oh, the hat!' Alex remembered on their way out the door. She ran back into her room and found the old black fedora in her closet, plunked it on top of her Heidi wig, and returned to Vera. They headed up the street to the tube station.

As they sat in their seats on the tube, they were already into character. They'd discussed it in detail before and decided that they'd have to be in character from the beginning or else they wouldn't be able to go through with the whole thing. Once they entered Tufnell Park Station, the performance had begun. The main thing, above all, was for them to act as if this was how they really were. As if they always looked like this, as if Vera always wore pink silk kimonos with embroidered gold crane designs over a purple sweatsuit with turquoise Reebok hightops. As if Alex always wore the navy blue pleated skirt from Marks and Spencer's over long green thermal leggings and a yellow peasant shirt stuffed with old socks just above the waist to make it look like an old lady's sagging breasts.

Between Camden Town and Euston Alex leaned over to Vera. 'I think my tits have all shifted to the left side,' she whispered, pulling her down vest tighter around her. Vera's eyes lit in laughter, but other than that she didn't crack a smile.

At Leicester Square they left the Northern Line and headed for the Piccadilly. Alex's tap shoes echoed loudly as they walked through the passageway. On their way up the escalator they caught sight of a couple blatantly staring at them. Everyone was staring, but in typical English fashion, most people cast their eyes aside when Vera or Alex caught them looking.

'Shall we speak pig-Latin from here on out?' Alex whispered to Vera.

'Es-yay,' Vera answered. They both maintained solemn expressions as if they'd just arrived off the boat and had to find a place to sleep that night.

On the Piccadilly Alex asked Vera, 'Ut-whay oo-day ou-yay ink-thay ee-way ould-shay art-stay ith-way?'

'Ady-lay of-way Ain-spa,' Vera answered.

'Eally-ray?' reacted Alex, not sure. Vera nodded. The British Telecom employee sitting across from them quickly looked up at the Poems on the Underground poster above his seat. The lady across the aisle with the Harrod's bag, drew the bag closer to her and suddenly found a piece of lint on her skirt to brush off.

At Covent Garden they walked through the crowds almost unnoticed and headed for the mall area. Outside three Irish folksingers were doing their rendition of a Chieftains number and a small crowd was assembled around them. Alex couldn't resist and shuffled her tap shoes loudly as they passed by. She waved as people from the crowd turned and looked.

They went around to the other side of the mall area. A pool of people were gathered around a mime who was knocking on a non-existent door. They went a little further over, then dropped their things down in the middle of an open space.

'I want where he is,' Vera whined, pointing at the mime.

'He'll leave eventually, then we'll move over there,' Alex replied, optimistically, as she pulled out her castanets and took off her down jacket. Vera began the task of getting her accordion out of its case. Overhead, clouds were beginning to move swiftly.

'It'll probably start pissing with rain,' Vera said nervously.

'Well, at least it won't ruin our hairdos,' Alex snickered as she reached over and adjusted Vera's wig. Vera put the strap of the accordion around her neck, closed the case, adjusted the instrument in position, put one foot up on the case and started warming up. A few people began noticing them. Alex did some knee bends and flexed each foot a few times, working out any stiffness, letting the taps on the shoes loosen up. After several minutes they looked at each other, Alex took the hat off her head, put in a few coins, and placed it on the ground in front of them. Alex took her position, put her hands on her hips, and they nodded to each other.

'Lady of Spain I adore you,' they started singing after Vera's introductory chords, 'Lady of Spain I implore you.' Their voices were strained at first, needing to get warmed up, but by the second round of the Lady of Spain refrain they were belting it out. Six or seven people had wandered over and were displaying a mixed-bag of expressions. What started out as mild curiosity led to embarrassed amusement, then, when they realized it was safe to laugh, assorted chuckles began and, eventually, a loud chorus of laughter. Coins began to clink into the black hat as Alex tapped her way around Vera, her hands held high, the castanets clicking away.

After a brief pause for applause, Vera whispered 'Jealousy'. Alex reached over and pulled a black scarf and a plastic red rose from her Sainsbury's bag. She draped the scarf across her chin and stuck the rose in her mouth. A few bars into Vera's music, she vamped into the crowd of people and targeted a fiftyish American man as her victim. She tapped around him, throwing her scarf around his face, winking and making suggestive expressions with her eyes, rubbing her shoulder up against his chest as his wife stood next to him, tears of laughter rolling down her cheeks. By now there were twenty or thirty people watching, laughing at their act, pointing at the various items of clothing they were wearing. Coins clinked into the hat.

As the people applauded the number, Vera adjusted the accordion strap, stepped around the case and plunked her other foot upon it. In the meantime, Alex, in full view of the audience, adjusted her sock-tits and rolled her eyes up into her head as if to indicate exasperation.

By the time Vera cut into their Sinatra 'My Way' routine, all the red stars had come off Alex's tap shoes. A little girl from the crowd periodically ran out and collected another one which had fallen off. Light drops of rain started to fall and some of the people in the audience began to stray away.

'I don't know,' Vera said over the cappuccino. 'If we only had a way to take a chair with us so I could sit down.' Her feet were killing her. Alex positioned her chair behind Vera and tried to massage her shoulders. Their wigs lay on the table; wet red ringlets on top of wet yellow plaits. Alex plucked at her own salt and pepper locks. Vera smoothed back the sides of her hair.

'Well, almost sixteen quid in an hour ain't bad,' Alex sighed, moving her chair back in place. 'It ain't art but it ain't bad,' she said.

'Yeah, but . . .' Vera sipped her coffee.

'Beats typing,' Alex said, 'or stuffing envelopes,' she added, 'or waiting tables.' She suddenly found she'd run out of things that busking beat. They were both exhausted. Neither looked at the other.

'Well, I don't know about you, but I'm swiftly sinking into my "When-will-my-Prince-come-along mode".' Vera said eventually.

'We got rid of royalty in my kingdom,' Alex snapped indignantly, crinkling her upper lip. 'But I guess we really are a little too old for this,' she conceded to Vera's bedraggled expression.

'A *little*!'

'I guess we just have to face it,' Alex continued, ignoring Vera's increasing hostility and gathering up her wig, stuffing it into her backpack and standing. 'We're too old to start again and too young to draw a pension.' She put on her down jacket and handed the other wig to Vera. 'I guess we just gotta keep moving sideways till we find a crack.'

They allowed a sigh to pass between them then, each

recognizing the depressed mood they had plunged into, then they headed out of the café and back towards the tube station.

When the tube stopped at Tottenham Court Road Alex turned to Vera.

'I was just thinking . . .' she said, and Vera darted a look at her that could have killed. It had been Alex's idea for them to busk, and look where that had gotten them.

'Maybe we could come up with enough money to go to Avebury next weekend,' Alex continued, oblivious of Vera's expression. 'We could take some bags with us and pick up a bunch of rocks and put an advert in some holistic magazine in the States and sell these rocks as ancient power stones from the Druids.'

Vera's eyes lit ever-so-slightly at Alex's new idea.

'Hmm,' she answered.

'We could mount them on 14-carat gold necklaces,' Alex waxed, 'and each one could come with its own little Celtic prayer.' Alex thought a minute. 'Were Druids Celts?' she asked Vera.

'Beats me,' Vera answered. The two continued to think about the new plan as they rode along in silence.

'No,' Vera finally said. 'It won't work. Americans don't know about that kind of thing. And what's more, they don't give a shit. Even the New Age type Americans. All Americans want is to be saved. Unless this is gonna save 'em in some way, you can forget it.'

'Yeah,' mumbled Alex, 'I guess you're probably right. Saved.'

'Saved. To live happily ever after. Amen.'

Vera and Alex said nothing as they exited the Tufnell Park station. They walked silently down Tufnell Park Road, headed towards home. Each seemed to be trying to remember something. Something that could save them. Some kind of prayer, Celtic or otherwise, that they could say. Any kind of prayer that might do the trick.

Troglodytes

Lizzie was a true yellow rose of Texas who still said words like 'ya'll' when she didn't catch herself first. 'Ya'll 're just puttin' me on, right?' she'd say, then correct herself quickly with 'I mean, you're just kidding me, aren't you?' She'd slip and use the word 'where' instead of the phrase 'so that'. 'I always listen to the Eagles where I won't get homesick,' she'd say. 'Just let me finish cuttin' up these onions where I can put them in the tuna salad.' She practiced saying 'wash' over and over again, listening to the sound to make sure she wasn't saying 'warsh.' She concentrated on aspirating her ts. She worked on her diphthongs and spoke to herself in the mirror each morning to see if her nose moved. If her nose moved she knew she was talking too nasally.

Now that she'd moved here she never knew where she was anymore because the sun arced on the horizon instead of directly overhead like it should. The streets curled and wandered instead of going straight in a grid. When people gave directions they never used the word 'blocks' but instead said things like 'three streets along.' As a result, Lizzie felt she was at the mercy of strangers and, for once, knew how Blanche Dubois felt in 'A Streetcar Named Desire'.

But the strangers turned out to be *really* strange. Like they'd originally been creatures with shells and had somehow evolved over the eons so that now the actual shells had become invisible, but they didn't know it. It always took her a while each day to remember this fact; that people weren't going to make eye contact with her or speak to her when she walked down the street. After passing a few people she'd remember not to look in their faces anymore, but straight ahead as if going towards God.

But neither God nor the mercy of strangers had been much help when he'd kicked her out.

When he'd kicked her out he hadn't been friendly about it. Actually, uncouth was the word for it, he'd been downright uncouth. Over the years, she'd experienced her share of emotional retardees, played Wendy to a few Peter Pans and watched a couple of angry young men grow old overnight, but in all her sweet days she'd never seen the lights go out quite as dark and fast as the way he made them.

She'd met him in Austin at the El Azteca Café. She'd been gorging herself on her weekly dose of cheese enchiladas with red chillis and sour cream when he'd come in and sat down at the booth next to where she and her friend, Carlene, were seated. They heard him talking to the waitress. British, they'd mouthed to each other. An English accent. Everything about him looked foreign and exciting, like some kind of rock star. His hair was spiked on top, cut in a way you never saw in Austin, a foreign, sexy way like David Bowie's in the early eighties or something, and he wore a faded green denim vest over a shirt that looked western, but not on him. Eventually, as if on a dare from Carlene, she leaned over and said, 'You from England?' and smiled her shit-eating grin. One thing led to another and she'd found herself showing him around, taking him to Bad Frank's for a few beers, making out with him on a blanket by the lake, getting chigger bites all over her back as a result.

It had been what you might call a whirlwind romance, a veritable tornado of love coming out of nowhere, picking them up and depositing them on the shores of what-do-we-do-now? As it turned out, he wanted a green card so he could work in the States so, feeling like destiny had reached out of nowhere and struck her between the eyes, she married him. But six months later he got depressed and homesick, so they sold all her things and, on the money they got, split for England. 'For richer for poorer' she piously quoted to herself from her marriage vows whenever she had second thoughts about using her money to get them over here. She wasn't raised a Southern Baptist for nothing.

Then one day, seven or eight months after they'd settled in London, when she came home from working her evening cleaning shift at Debenham's, she walked over to him as he stood at the kitchen sink and put her arms around his waist to give him a hug. He pulled away and moved over to the fridge. He took out her jar of pickled okra and put it in a Safeway bag. He took the stack of frozen tortillas out of the freezer and her package of Oreos, a package of pinto beans and the bag of cornmeal out of the cabinet and put them in the bag. He added the jar of salsa but, she noticed, he left out the bottle of tequila.

'This should get you started,' he said.

'Started?'

'In your new place.'

'What new place?'

'The one you find without me in it.'

It had taken two weeks of looking in the classifieds and going to various houses to check out the rooms before she'd managed to find a place. In the meantime he disappeared, giving no further explanation. He'd come back to the flat when she was at work and leave notes like, 'The phone bill arrived. Your part is £57. Please do not make anymore foreign phone calls before you move.'

Fred had spent the last five years in Paris working with André Jourdain who had been a star pupil and devotee of the mime god, Etienne Decroux. Fred had learned to control every muscle of his body, every bone, being able to demonstrate at the drop of a hat his ability to make his body behave like a puppet on the strings of his mind. But André suddenly moved to Quebec, his students dispersed, and Fred, tired of Europe but not feeling inclined or ready to go back home to Minneapolis, decided to wander over to London.

At first he'd tried busking in Covent Garden. But people looked at him like he was a creature from a Cronenberg horror film. These audiences wanted their mimes to have white faces, spider-drawn eyes and teardrops on their cheeks. They wanted to see walls created with white-gloved hands. When he started moving the various parts of his body to demonstrate his control, they at least expected it to lead into some kind of break-dancing routine. They were not in the least entertained.

He heard about the room in the flat in Archway from a sign that was posted in the cappuccino bar on Neal Street where he'd got a job waiting tables. The guy who was advertising the room was an art student, and he was moving in with his girlfriend. Fred agreed to take the room immediately and asked the student if he might be able to occupy right away. He spent three nights sleeping on the kitchen floor, waking to portraits in oil of people, friends of the artist supposedly, whom he hoped he'd never have to meet. The student finally moved out and took his paintings. Thankfully, he didn't introduce Fred to any of his friends.

As it turned out, the woman who had shared the flat with the artist/student decided to move out a week after the student did. She'd broken up with her boyfriend, played a Jane's Addiction tape over and over (it had been 'their' record), and the only times Fred ever saw her were when she'd come into the kitchen to make herself another cup of Morning Surprise tea. When she left she took the kettle, the Moulinex blender/coffee grinder, the television set and the tape deck. Luckily, she also took her Jane's Addiction tape.

'I'm afraid we're a little lacking in the finer comforts of life,' he apologized to Lizzie about the absence of appliances as he showed her around the flat. He noticed she didn't say much, that the bottom of her eyes had red semi-circles.

'I suppose you don't allow smokers?' she said defeatedly as though she were waiting to be rejected.

'Only if they smoke something stronger than these Light Silk Cuts.' He reached over to where his jacket hung on a peg in the hallway and lifted his pack of cigarettes out. He took one, then offered one to her. She smiled gratefully.

'I have to get up real early every morning to clean at Debenham's, then I have to go back at night.' She said this as if it were a factor even more damning than the smoking.

'You work at Debenham's?'

'I clean there. Five mornings and evenings a week. They have a different staff at the weekend.'

'Wow! Does that mean you could maybe pick up a few things, you know, pinch the occasional trash bag, I mean bin liner as they call it here ... you know, the random cleaning product? Those things add up you know. With me bringing home the occasional scrap from the coffee bar, we could cut corners no end.'

'So this old man's at another window in the post office and he's yelling "I can't hear a bloody word you're saying,' and the guy on the other side of the window says something else and all the other postal clerks on the inside laugh and all the people in my queue start shifting their feet and giving each other these amused little looks. It goes on like this the whole time I'm in the queue and the old man's getting more and more upset. So, I finally get my stamps and, since no one else is doing anything, and since the post office clerks are just shaking their heads and mumbling to themselves behind their glass, I go over to the old man and I ask if I can help him.

"What?" he snaps at me. He's real mad by now.

"Can I help at all?" I say.

"What?" he yells louder. "I can't hear a bloody word you're saying." He turned back to the guy at the window and started in on him again, so I just left. But everybody stared at me as I walked out the door.'

'That'll teach you,' Fred said, lighting a cigarette as they strolled along the South Bank of the river and crossed Waterloo Bridge. 'Maybe now you'll learn not to try to be so helpful. People don't like that here. It makes them think you think they're bad by not offering to help too. They feel guilty and confused, which of course they are, but they don't like being made to feel that way. They like to go about their lives thinking that God has a BBC accent and everything is "perfect really, thank you."'

Lizzie and Fred had arranged to meet after they each got off work. After several months of coming home each night, tired and drained, they'd grown bored with Scrabble, frustrated in their attempts to get a few answers to the *Guardian* crossword, and they'd taken to bringing books home from the library and reading to each other. Last week Lizzie had read Fred a Tony Hillerman thriller, but this week, for some ungodly reason Fred had chosen Plato. Out of all the books in all the world he'd brought home a collection of Plato's works and proceeded to read the one about the man in the cave. It was OK really, not exactly what she enjoyed listening to the most, but interesting in a rather strange way. It was about a man who'd lived in a cave since he was little and another man came along and led him out. The man who's lived in the cave all this time can't believe what he sees around him and it blows his mind. It was an allegory, Fred explained, because it displayed in story-form the idea that each person is trapped inside his or her own little reality, own little cave-of-a-reality. It set Lizzie to thinking about things and the more she thought, the more disturbed she became. It seemed that she and Fred were getting more and more cave-like as the days went by so she finally suggested they needed to get out for a change. See what was out there, for god's sake. She'd been in London for almost a year and had been to Big Ben and the Houses of Parliament twice and that was about it.

They continued along the river and as they walked towards the Embankment tube station they were approached by more and more people asking for spare change. Others sat on the kerb, their hands permanently outstretched as though frozen in their stance of begging. One with a dog at his side, asked for money for dog food. An old lady sitting next to a trolley full of rags and odds and ends, said something totally indecipherable. As they approached the entry to the station a young woman with a small child sitting in a push-cart thrust her hand out in front of Lizzie.

'Spare some change for the baby?' she asked. Her eyes were glazed and her face was rife with red spots. The little boy's nose was running and he looked half asleep. Lizzie couldn't help thinking it wasn't just because it was his bedtime, but that he was suffering from malnutrition. She reached in the pocket of her jacket, pulled out her purse, and gave the woman a fifty-pence piece. The woman didn't thank her but quickly turned towards another passer-by and repeated her plea.

'They share the kid, you know,' Fred said as they slipped their tickets into the slots to enter the turnstile of the tube.

'What?'

'Those women,' he continued, 'I've heard they have shifts. One of them has a kid you see, and a bunch of them trade off. Each one takes him for a few hours to beg with. They get better money that way.'

'But that's horrible!' Lizzie said, outraged. 'What about the little boy?'

'Well, it's not as though they can put him in any kind of child care, can they?' They were silent for a few minutes as they made their way towards the platform. Once there they sat down and stared at the advertisement that was plastered on the wall across from them. It was a tourist advert, one that proclaimed the glories of vacationing in the Caribbean. Another one, next to it, promoted the benefits of a private health care scheme.

'Well, what would you do then?' Fred asked. 'If you had a kid and no money, no husband and no place to live, no job, no skills, a major recession going on . . .'

Lizzie thought for a moment. 'Well, for one thing, I'd get outta here.'

'Yeah, right. Where?'

'Home. I'd go home.'

'You mean the States, right? They've got homeless people in the States too, you know. Lots of them from what I hear. But, anyway, they don't have that option, they're British.' Fred didn't look at her as the train came in and they got on. They rode in silence for a while.

'But why don't they go home, back to where they came from?' she asked as though the conversation had been going on the whole time.

Fred shot her an exasperated look. 'Talk about The Allegory of the Cave! Where've you been?' He looked around helplessly, searching for where to start, what explanation to throw at her first. She wasn't stupid, but it seemed to him she suffered from terminal greenness and he couldn't imagine how she'd managed to survive and live in this city for almost a year and not know more than this. His irritation was assuaged by a sudden conclusion.

'Is it because you're from Texas, is that it? That must be it. Texans think there's always an easy answer.'

'What do you know about Texans?' she became defensive, then she caught herself and thought about it. Maybe that *was* the reason. At home whenever times had got rough in the past, you just went out and did something else. Even before she'd left, with the recession going on and people getting fired and things costing so much more, she'd still been able to find a way to make ends meet. Maybe it was different here. Maybe there weren't as many choices. Her mind swirled in trying to figure it out.

'Well, look, I may not know much about Texans,' Fred conceded, 'but you've got to stop putting such easy answers on things. There's just too much you don't know about to be taken into consideration.'

It wasn't exactly Fred's words that did it, it was everything. Thoughts, sensations and the night's revelations swirled together and crystalized themselves into a tiny pinpoint of a realization. It didn't take long. In fact, by the time they'd reached Archway, exited the tube and started walking down the hill towards their flat, Lizzie had decided. She felt her steps come down firmly on the pavement, felt her shoulders actually relax for the first time in days as she looked up at the hazy night sky. Mercury could just barely be seen and the moon was almost full.

'Well, they may not be able to, but I can,' she said to him as though he'd been in on the conversation going on inside her mind.

'They may not be able to what, but you can?' His mind boggled.

'Go home!' She stopped and spread her arms out as if to welcome the air. He looked at her and smiled.

'That was quick. But, in a way, it took you long enough.'

She looked at him and wondered what he meant.

'I mean, it didn't take you long to make up your mind once you started thinking about it. But what I wonder is why it took you so long to think about it in the first place?'

They continued walking and she thought about what he'd said.

'Patty Hearst Syndrome,' she said, once again, out of the blue.

'What?'

'I suffered from the Patty Hearst Syndrome. You know, captured and brainwashed into thinking that this was who I was, that destiny had led me to this? That's why it took me so long to see I needed to go home.'

Fred laughed as they entered the flat. 'Well, at least Patty Hearst had a few bucks behind her to get her out of *her* mess.

How're you going to handle it?' They both looked around the sitting room of the flat. The sofa was littered with yesterday's *Guardian* and the Scrabble game sat at the edge of it. In the kitchen a single pan, unwashed since supper, sat on the cooker and a few dishes were stacked in the kitchen sink. It was the first time Lizzie had really looked at her situation and what she saw wasn't very comforting. She went over to the sofa and collapsed into it. Suddenly everything looked crushed and hopeless. Fred watched as she took it all in. She was beyond green. She was the first primordial speck of algae to appear upon the surface of the earth. He went over and sat down on the sofa next to her. Unable to fathom what the hell she'd occupied her mind with over the last months, *ever* for that matter, he heaved a sigh.

'Well, I guess what you have to do first is find out how much it costs to get back.' He looked over at her and, considering her track-record so far, wondered if she'd even be able to do that. 'There's this student place near work where they sell cheap tickets. Maybe you could go there and check it out.'

She looked at him, the daze on her face was still there, but with a new concern breaking through it.

'What about you?'

'Me?' He rolled his eyes up into his head and rubbed his hands through his hair. 'Oh god, me.' He reached into his jacket and pulled out a cigarette, lit it. 'Let's just not talk about me for now, OK? I mean, it's bad enough we have to talk about you.'

'But why don't you go home too?'

He inhaled a drag off the cigarette and let the smoke out slowly. He looked around the room, at the cracks coming down one of the walls, the ratty brown carpet, the peeling paint on the radiator. 'Let's just say I like it here,' he finally uttered, an ironic smile barely showing itself beneath the surface of his face. 'So many places to go, people to see, things to do.' He looked over at her and laughed at her dismayed expression. 'OK, well then, maybe let's just say that I've always thrived on perversity.'

'Perversity?'

He saw that she had no way of understanding where he was coming from. 'Look,' he gave in, 'I'm not ready, that's all. Besides, there's nothing drawing me back. I left to go to Paris *for* something. But in this case, destiny doesn't call me, as you might put it.' He reached over and tousled her hair. 'Let's just focus on getting you back on the ranch, shall we?'

It was just before dark when they entered his flat. Lizzie had promised herself that she would not take stock of any signs of another woman's clothing or possessions. She would not grow nostalgic and morose if she saw his green denim vest hanging on the peg just inside the door, but would go straight to the task at hand. But, as it turned out, the signs were overwhelming, assaulting her as soon as they stepped through the door. There, on the other peg next to his vest, was a lady's cashmere coat and, on entering further into the room, she saw the vase of flowers, a new Habitat rug on the floor, and a tidiness about the place which he could never have managed. As she stood there looking around, Fred hurried over to the television, unplugged it and started coiling up the cord.

'What are you doing, for Christ's sake!' Fred hissed at her. 'We're not here for dinner, we're here to rip the bastard off, right?'

'Bastard!' she said, not simply repeating Fred's word, just saying it.

'Well, yeah, right, sure, come on then, we all know he's a bastard, nothing else is new, let's get the fuck out!' He went over to the stereo system and unplugged the cord from the power point. 'Here, you carry this, it's lighter.' She stood there, mesmerized by anger and frustration.

'He used all my money and . . .'

Fred walked over to her and grabbed her shoulders. 'Look, you're not Scarlett O'Hara and he's not the Yankees. You're here to get back your investment. And I'm not about to get caught

stealing and thrown in an English jail and be buggered by a
bunch of guys who all look like Oliver Reed and talk like Arthur
Scargill on methadone. Now come on!' He put the stereo in her
arms, picked up the television, and headed towards the door.

'Just a minute,' she said, and put the stereo down. She
quickly headed for the bedroom and, without stopping to look
around, opened the door of the clothes cupboard. Ignoring the
dresses and other items of women's clothing which now hung
where hers used to hang, she pulled out his shirts, his pair of
black jeans, and every other thing that looked like his, slung
them over her arm and headed back to the front room. Then she
picked up the stereo and followed Fred out the door, not
looking back.

She had managed to cram everything into just two suitcases and
two carry-on bags. She had bought ten packages of Polos and a
half dozen Bournevilles for the flight over, since she'd decided
to give up smoking. Fred had announced that he was treating
her to a mini-cab and was coming along for the ride.

On Friday, Fred had come home with three hundred pounds
and a cassette recorder/radio ghetto blaster. He said the guy
he'd sold the stuff to only had that much money but had thrown
in the ghetto blaster as a sweetener. She'd been hoping for £350,
but when she saw Fred's face light up as he turned the radio on
and started playing with the dial, she realized it was only fair that
he get something out of the deal. Besides, she liked thinking
that she could remember him this way, with something to do
besides play Scrabble or do crosswords with his next flat-mate.

As planned, they got out of the mini-cab at the station where
they'd seen all the homeless people. Fred carried the heavy
suitcases and Lizzie her carry-on bags. As they headed towards
the beggars Lizzie motioned to Fred.

'Wait here, OK?' Fred smiled at her as he put down the
suitcases, leaned against the wall of a building and looked at his
watch. They'd timed it just right. After she did her thing they'd

have just enough time to hail another taxi and make it to the airport.

'If you're not back in ten minutes I'll see you in the next life, OK?' he said as they exchanged grins.

As Lizzie walked close to the overpass where a cardboard city was set up, the street people seemed to come out of the woodwork. She soon saw the old lady with the trolley and the young woman, only a different one this time, with the little boy in the push-cart. Their hands reached out as if under water, their mouths bubbling words that couldn't make it to the surface. She started reaching into the bag.

She gave the old lady his brown and black cowboy shirt and the man with the dog his black jeans. She started at one side of the tunnel where the caves of cardboard began, then circled back on the other side when she came to the end. She pulled out his red football jersey, his white shirt for dressing up, the turquoise corduroy (the one which had always made his eyes look like he wore colored contacts), the blue and black lumberjack shirt, the loose Mexican pullover. She didn't look at their faces, didn't listen for responses. She knew they'd rather have money, beer, something else. But she couldn't give them anything else. She only had this.

Back to religion

'I think I could live in Italy, even without friends, even with the language problem,' Lee said, 'if I were in love and had enough money to have a house with one room that stayed empty and white.' She clipped her big toenail and put the cutting into the yellow plastic Ricard ashtray she'd stolen from the pub the night before.

'You always were bourgie,' said Dana, still wearing ruffled blouses at age forty-six.

'Bourgie, nothing! I was always *romantic*,' Lee answered, as she contorted her middle-aged body into a position that made it possible for her to work on the other big toenail.

'Bourgie. We are both just as middle-class bourgeois as we ever were in spite of the epiphanies and ecstasies and writhings that our destined meteoric experiences have wrought.' Dana took a sip of her margarita and picked up the *New Statesman*, flipping through it as if it were a fashion magazine. She'd been visiting Lee here in London for the last week and it had already become just like old times.

'So, where could *you* live then, other than L.A.?' Lee figured that Dana would probably come up with something like a self-contained glass bubble on Mars. 'And under what conditions?' She took off her turquoise and agate rings and her yellow-faced designer watch and placed them on the table beside her.

'New York maybe,' Dana said distractedly, glancing judgementally at the small abstract expressionist painting on Lee's wall. 'If I had a good shrink and a steady supply of clean coke.' She got up and straightened the painting, sat down again. She added an afterthought: 'And enough money to take taxis all the time.'

'Talkin' about bourgeois,' said Lee, lighting a cigarette.

'Well, I never said I wasn't.'

'Ah, come on, are you kidding? You used to go on for hours about it. All about how you come from a long line of lefty Jewish atheists and how that gave you insights into the human condition that made you different from everyone else. For instance, back in '63, remember how you'd get all hot and bothered about anyone who was crazy about Ingmar Bergman? You'd say anyone who thought Ingmar Bergman was God, was just an elitist unoriginal pseudo-intellectual. Then later – must have been '64, '65 – you used to go into this whole lecture routine about how all the blacks in the south were getting to the place where all they really wanted, if the truth be known, was to become just like all the horribly corrupt middle-class whites. And always, no matter when it was, what year, what time of day, what season, you could always go on and on about how religion had manipulated the masses into subserviency to such an extent that if the Pope wanted them to eat each other they'd busily scratch around for a new sauce to marinate the meat in.' Lee plucked at her spiked hair as if to punctuate her words.

'Well, someone had to tell you all about it,' Dana said.

Lee narrowed her eyes into a squint, pretending hostility. Then the two laughed at each other in recognition of their old familiar ways of being with each other. 'I hate to admit it but I guess you're right,' Lee said. Dana and Lee had sparred like this since college when Dana was the Jew of the drama department and Lee was learning not to be the Gentile.

'I mean, you were so green I figured that cross you always wore was probably made out of brass,' Dana kept on.

Lee chuckled at the memory of herself in those days. Back

then she was the good Southern Baptist girl her mother had always wanted.

'I stopped wearing it after I met you,' Lee said.

Dana rolled her eyes up towards the flaming red hair that dangled across her forehead.

'You're saying *I* was the cause of your downfall?'

'Been going down ever since.'

'Into the mouths of?'

'The very gaping ones.' Lee put salt on her hand, bit at a slice of lime and picked up her tequila. Then she tucked her feet under her and held her glass up to Dana.

'To fallen angels,' she toasted.

'May their crumpled wings find a stiff breeze,' Dana flourished.

'Or may those wings fall off and our feet grow calluses from walking on paths of gold.'

'Bullshit,' said Dana, 'I wanna fly, goddamn it!' Dana sat up erect in her seat, arms outstretched.

Lee gave Dana a look that said she could have predicted such a reply. 'You always did. Haven't you learned yet?' she said.

'Learned to fly? Or learned not to want to?' Dana said. 'Your use of language always was a bit mystifying.'

'I know,' answered Lee. 'I always trusted that people close to me would be sensitive enough to understand what I was saying.'

'Well, haven't *you* learned yet, peachums?' Dana retorted, pouring a shot of straight tequila into her glass.

'Constantly.'

'What?'

'What do you mean, "What?"'

'What . . . have . . . you . . . learned?' Dana drew each word out slowly, as if to a child. She sometimes had a difficult time dealing with these conversations with Lee that somehow eventually ended up resembling bad Beckett.

Lee paused a moment, contemplating her answer. She reflected that one never knew when a question like this could turn into some kind of philosophical or religious discussion with all sorts of rhetoric and analysis that she didn't really want to get into.

'To keep trying, I guess. To just keep trying to trust.'

'Oh, god.' Dana collapsed back into her chair and took a big swig of her drink. 'You lived in California too long.'

'Me? You still live there. I'm the one who lives here.'

'Well, in that case, it's not a high recommendation of this place is it?'

They hiked upon the Heath as if they were in the Himalayas. As if they wore reinforced German paratrooper boots instead of Reeboks. As if wearing Reeboks made them athletic. Exercise had not been on their list of things they wanted to do when they each got older. They passed people walking dogs of all breeds.

'I miss my dog a lot,' Lee said sadly. 'Couldn't bring her because of the six-month quarantine they have here. I couldn't put her through that.'

Dana flashed no look of sympathy.

'You always were an animal person,' she finally said.

Lee remembered it was another category in which she and Dana differed dramatically.

'They're good for you, you should try them,' said Lee, who was never one to give up.

'Try what?'

'Animals!'

'You know I've been a vegetarian for just years,' Dana cackled at her bad joke. She saw Lee's exasperated look. 'Besides, most animals are hairy. It's bad enough I have to shave my legs.'

'You don't have to,' Lee said.

'I don't have to what? Get an animal or shave my legs?'

'Shave your legs.'

'Well, I do if I'm ever gonna get any more pornos. Directors of pornographic cinema prefer clean shaves on their women. The men can be apes.'

'Oh, come on, you haven't done that for years,' Lee said disgustedly, knowing that Dana was only using this reference to those few porno films she'd done in the early seventies just to stir her up again.

'True. But I prefer to keep up the image.' Dana clutched her fake leopard-skin coat to her neck. 'Christ, it gets colder 'an shit here!' she said, gritting her perfectly capped teeth.

'You ain't seen nothin',' Lee said. 'These days I look forward to menopause. Give me some of them hot flashes is what I say.'

'Hell, not me. I'm skipping menopause. Straight into non-hormonal old age for me. I'll start to wear head scarves any day now.' Dana's hennaed hair curled five inches out from her smallish face. It was hard to imagine her in head scarves.

'I think I'll carry a pearl-handled cane,' Lee fantasized. 'Really though, I think it would actually have to be a shepherd's staff because of my height. You know, one with notches carved on it, one for each lover.'

'God!' croaked Dana, 'I'd have to carry a bundle of canes if that were the case.'

Lee thought of the list of seventy-three-and-one-half lovers that Dana had written in one of her journals. Dana had shown it to her once when they'd both lived in L.A. She'd recorded each lover's name over the years. Lee wondered what the score was by now. Then she remembered the half.

'By the way, remember that list you used to have in your journal? The one with all the names of your past lovers that you showed me? I think you had seventy-three-and-a-half or something like that.' Lee paused a moment to reconsider whether or not she really wanted to ask the question, then her curiosity finally got the best of her. 'Well, what I always wondered was, what did the half mean?'

Dana looked at Lee, trying to figure out what she was talking about, then it clicked. 'Oh. Well, you see, it doesn't count if they don't come,' she explained.

'Oh. Really?' Lee paused to reflect upon the implications of that, and began to re-count to herself. 'Well then, that cuts mine down to about fourteen.'

'What, twenty-eight guys who never came or thirteen who did and two who didn't?' asked Dana who always was quick with arithmetic.

'Thirteen and two,' answered Lee, embarrassed.

'Such a novice.'

'Well, not exactly a nun.'

'It all goes back to religion in life doesn't it?' Dana pointed out.

They arrived at a hill where five or six kites were racing across the sky.

'I had a friend once who designed this kite,' said Dana. 'It was this large neon green condom thing with puce-coloured scarves trailing from the end for its tail. But he couldn't get it off the ground so he decided that this was a symbol of his own virility, or lack thereof, and that perhaps he should have a sex change.'

'Interesting logic,' Lee said. Two young men were walking towards them on the other side of the path and something about the way they moved and looked at each other caught Lee's attention. She moved closer to Dana and took her arm.

'Now's not the time, for god's sake. After all these years you now, all at once, decide to turn bi on me just because you've realized you've only had fourteen lovers. Well, thirteen-and-two-halves.' Dana pinched Lee's cheek with affection. One of the men Lee had noticed suddenly lurched after Dana's handbag which was slung over her shoulder, while the other knocked Lee down, grabbed her bag and started to run. Lee sprang back up, and seeing that Dana was managing a kick defense towards her assailant, sprinted off in pursuit of her purse-snatcher.

'The eyes!' she screamed back at Dana. 'Go for his eyes!'

'Eyes, shit! It's the teeny goddamn marble-sized fuckin'

balls . . .' Dana screeched as she grabbed the man's coat and held on for dear life, thrusting her knees into every available place of his body she could reach.

'Thank god they were such wimps,' Lee said in relief as she strewed the possessions of her handbag out in front of her on the floor of her living room.

'Speak for yourself,' said Dana. 'It's about time those hundreds of dollars of Karate lessons paid off. I'd a preferred a hulk really. Some primordial ape type with a neck the size of a redwood trunk to sink my teeth into.' She was putting her things back into her bag. Lee noticed the blue plastic container.

'You don't actually carry a diaphragm around with you do you?'

'Of course. Gives me the illusion that I might need to use it sometime before I get around to buying a new bag.' She dropped it back into the bag. 'Besides, if I die, and they return my final effects to my mother, I want to make sure she has something to get upset about.'

'She wouldn't be. Not after all these years.'

'No. But it gives me another illusion. I'm really getting into illusions lately. I'm becoming more attached to Cocteau's "it's all done with mirrors" as the days go by.'

One of Lee's knees was bruised from her tumble with the attacker and she hobbled like an old lady as she got up and went into the kitchen to make tea.

'God, it looks like you could really use that cane you were talking about earlier,' noticed Dana.

'I'd have liked to have used it earlier on those guys,' Lee answered, rubbing her knee. 'Hey, how come you're not all sore too?'

Dana thought about it for a moment.

'Well, there's only one reason I can think of really. It must be because I'm Jewish. What d'ya think?'

Clarissa finds the way

When Clarissa came back from the Casa d'Or she weighed twenty pounds less, had an aquiline nose, a firm thirty-seven-inch bustline, no stretch marks, a month's supply of high-potency zinc and iron chelate and no husband. She had two children gone away to college, a degree in comparative religions, a mantra, an exercise schedule, a year's membership at the Third Eye Centre, and a sizeable monthly alimony check. Her astrological chart had been progressed up through the next six months. But, unfortunately, the last Tarot reading had seen the card which concerns matters of the heart come out upside down.

Her shrink, whom she'd been seeing on and off for seven years, and Koto, the guru from whom she'd been taking classes in meditation for three years, each agreed with her that it might be to her mental and spiritual advantage if she found something constructive to do with her extra time. *What* was another question. In looking around for an idea of something she could do, she became aware of the fact that all her friends constantly complained about how they just couldn't get good 'help' anymore. So, she started a cleaning service. She hired ten people to do the work and an accountant to do the books. She made $75,000 in a year, gave a sizeable amount of it to the Third Eye Centre, paid off her shrink and sold the business for a handsome profit.

Somehow, the business just hadn't been spiritually fulfilling.

Ralph, however, was. Because of Ralph she could now meditate an hour each day. She no longer felt a need for eating meat, she could read French surrealist poetry and actually relate to it, and she could wear purple for the first time in her life. Because of Ralph she could now live without her Clinique eyeshadow and actually look at pictures of herself taken before her nose job. She could feel true solidarity with her sisters in third-world countries. She was even satisfied with driving a three-year-old BMW instead of needing to get a new one every year, like her ex-husband had always done, and she felt relatively enlightened on the subject of the legalization of marijuana when it came up in discussion at dinner parties.

Ralph had been such a god-send. She had met him at the Third Eye Centre where he'd been conducting a seminar on aromatherapy. The inner calm that his voice had projected along with the spring-like aura of his clear blue eyes seemed to transcend the material world. These qualities had bathed her spirit in an ethereal nectar.

And, as it turned out, his body had stimulated chakras in her body she had never known existed before.

That first week with him his clarity of spirit and his minimalist life-style had humbled her and made her reflect upon her own way of living. She had considered selling her car, selling her house, putting her possessions in storage, and hitting the road with Ralph in his VW bus. But he had convinced her that material goods could be used in ways that could enhance and stimulate one's spiritual growth. So, instead, Ralph had moved in. She had been inspired by his innate ability to rearrange their environment in more aesthetically pleasing and psychically-attuned ways. The abstract-expressionist painting that had resided prominently in the entry hall had been replaced by the Tibetan thanka which Ralph had discovered and she had bought at a steal for only $1,500. The white chintz living room sofa and chairs had been transformed by the Afghani hand-woven blankets he'd found and she'd bought for a thousand-dollar-each song.

Six months and forty-thousand dollars later, Ralph left for a trek to Nepal, on an open round-the-world ticket financed by the sale of the thanka and the Afghani blankets. She'd arrived home from her class in radionics to find the thanka and blankets gone and a note on the hall table:

> Life is like a tree. The people encountered along one's
> way are like leaves. There is a season to everything in
> one's life, just as with trees. I feel it is now the autumn
> of our relationship and our leaves must thus be shed. I
> shall think of you often as you and I enter new seasons.
> You, yours, me, mine.

Unfortunately, a few days after he had left, Clarissa found out that his tree apparently had relatively quick seasons; somehow it had managed to skip winter, and was well into spring, because he was actively pollinating a twenty-two-year-old graduate student from Claremont who was accompanying him on his trip.

After a few weeks of going back into intensive therapy, Clarissa decided to take her own trip. She and her shrink discussed that doing such a thing was perhaps a form of escapism, but they came to the conclusion that escapism was credible if one recognized that it was escapism.

She packed all the light-weight clothing she owned that was not purple and flew to New Orleans, took a room at the Charles and ate meat for the first time in over six months. It was only fish however, a creole gumbo couldn't be that damaging to one's aura. She decided to take a vacation from meditation as well and, instead, drank a half-litre bottle of sauvignon blanc and four tequila sunrises in the hotel's bar before returning to her room at midnight with a Québecois Canadian who made his living by delivering boats to their new owners in Costa Rica.

She did not spiritually transcend and only a few chakras were awakened.

Five days later she packed her newly-acquired Caribbean print sundresses and white Armani jacket, along with her other things, and flew to New York. Her old friend, Eve, whom she had phoned two nights before – after an unfortunate coupling with a man named Leather who spoke with an English accent and was in the States buying old English motorcycles to take back to England – had begged her to come for a visit. By the tone of Eve's voice when she had spoken to her and tried to fill her in on what had been going on, Clarissa knew that Eve probably thought she was falling apart. So, she figured she might as well take advantage of Eve's concern and be taken care of for a few days.

Eve consoled her like any old good friend of considerable financial means and prominent social position would do: she set up dinners with eligible bachelors, therapeutic trips to Berg-dorf's, and appointments with Dr Frank, her own psychothera-pist – a good shrink still did wonders, god knows. Three weeks later Clarissa made phone calls back home in California, arranging to have her house put on the market, the car sold and her things sent to her new apartment just three blocks away from Eve.

Life was so miraculous, wasn't it?

The people at the New York New Age Centre were different from those she'd known back home in California at the Third Eye Centre; they were either old hippy types or extremely young novitiates of the most serious sort, so Clarissa abandoned tuning into them. Instead, she turned her attentions towards integrat-ing her spiritual side with the outside world. She joined a culinary group which adopted themes such as 'Crustaceans of the Month'. She went to concerts of commissioned works for computers and ensemble. She attended a few lectures at MOMA on post-minimalist art.

Although it was not particularly spiritually fulfilling, she did manage to enjoy a few weeks with Jorges, the computer ensemble composer. But, alas, Jorges turned out to prefer her company best when she sang 'I Got Plenty of Nuthin'' after he'd tied her to the bedstead with strings of pearls. When she eventually decided that his chakras were not aligned with hers, she suggested to him that it might be best that they shed the leaves of their relationship and try to plant new seeds elsewhere. He responded with a letter:

> I thought I should put pen to paper. Maybe it is appropriate and for the best that we should slip away from each other now, as you suggest. It's not without sadness that I watch you weigh anchor and depart on an unknown voyage. May the seas on which you sail be deep and full of wondrous revelation. Take advantage of the tide, sail far, sail wide. I wave farewell.

Not long after that she found Baxter who did amazing things with Cape Cod crab and performed like an octopus in bed. But, before any leaves had truly sprouted, he took a job as a chef on the QE II and sent her a note proclaiming she had been a wonderful experience and an interesting diversion from all those men he'd had over the years. Traumatized, she rushed to Dr Dubrecky, Eve's gynecologist, for an AIDS test. After all, it was what one had to do these days. To her overwhelming relief she tested negative and, in the process, she met Ian.

Ian had been at Dr Dubrecky's office with his sister who was also there for an AIDS test. She had tested negatively as well and, since she and Clarissa and Ian had shared an overwhelmingly psyche-damaging time in the waiting room of the doctor's office anticipating the results of the tests, they decided to celebrate their new lease on life. As it turned out, Ian taught two classes in post-minimalist art at the City College of New York. Teaching only part-time allowed him time to do his own art. His own art consisted of molding various-shaped mouths out of rubber sylastic, and motorizing the lips so that they could move. Then, on a rear-projected screen he showed films of people in the act of watching an assortment of films. He synchronized his molded lips with the mouth-reactions of the viewers of the movies. Clarissa thought Ian was a genius. She felt she might benefit in countless ways from exposure to such a profound person. But, unfortunately, Ian was obsessed with mouths in more ways than one, and Clarissa found she could not get her head, not to speak of her mouth, around that one. Besides, she was learning to practice safe sex now that she'd had such a scare about AIDS and Ian couldn't abide the aesthetics of condoms. Eventually, he sent her a letter after she'd announced to him that mouths could also be used for uttering words and the words she wanted to say to him were No No No:

> I'm disappointed in your lack of scope and
> perspective. I thought a woman of your experience and
> depth would have realized the importance of opening
> up to new dimensions. But, obviously, you are trapped
> in another period of expression which dictates
> parameters I no longer involve myself with. May the
> colors of your future vibrate with the shock of the
> new.

So, once again, Clarissa found herself alone, this time in her apartment on the Upper West Side of New York with nothing but her charge cards, three shelves of gourmet cookery books, a relatively reasonable bank account, two grown children who wrote letters from their ski trips to Aspen at Christmas, a standing appointment with Dr Frank, and a collection of letters from old lovers. Where, for god's sake, would it all end? What, for crying out loud, was it all about? Who among those Jungian gods she had grown to know and embrace could tell her what the fuck to do next? She sighed deeply, sighed again, then opened a bottle of Dom Perignon. She might as well make a toast to something. What on earth could she possibly toast now? Finally giving up on being able to think of anything to toast, she sat down on her raw silk-covered sofa and picked up the book she'd found at a local bookshop a few weeks before. She'd had no time to look at it then because of all the mess with Ian.

Relationships with unspiritual men had to be on her list of things to avoid from here on out, she told herself.

The book, 'Memorable Meetings with Remarkable Souls', was a series of interviews with New Age leaders from all over the world. She thumbed through it and stopped at the section on White Feather. White Feather was a medium who lived in the Pecos Wilderness near Santa Fé. White Feather was blessed with being able to channel Raging Bull, a Native American spirit who spoke through her from the other side. As Clarissa read further her hands began to tremble, her lips grew tight with excitement. This, by god, was it! The gods had shown her the very way, the very path to her destiny. How fortunate, how very lucky she was to be tuned in and open to the universal energy that would lead her towards her blossoming future.

All she had to do was to give herself up to it. Go with the flow.

There were not many bags to be packed. Just the Caribbean-print sundresses and the Armani jacket would do.

Trilobites

She walked like Sally Fields on valium. Her tits were the size of something red ants would have stung but they matched the rest of her body which could pass for sixteen on a beach at dusk with just the right light.

She gave up smoking at least twice a year and only the brown spots at the tips of her two front teeth gave her away if no one knew her habit. Skirts got caught in her stride so she always wore jeans or shorts. When she wanted to feel like a woman she shaved her legs. When she wanted to feel like a boy she didn't. When she wanted to feel like a girl she took smaller steps. She seldom wanted to feel like a man. When she wanted to feel like an old lady she picked flowers from other people's gardens at night as she walked down her street to the beach. She *never* wanted to feel like an old man.

The beach was why she lived where she did. The beach had that breeze that made the mimosa bloom, that grew the eucalyptus trees that dropped stars on the ground. The waves brought purple butterflies which flew away at night when no one was looking, leaving their shells behind on the beach. The air at the beach was like tequila with the lime already squeezed in. The Milky Way, seen from the beach, was a pure line of coke laid out on a clean mirror until somewhere around dawn you crept home to sleep and dream of pink.

He was the golden boy gone brown at the edges. His 'get-it-

now-or-don't-get-it-at-all' attitude had subsided with the on-
slaught of 'maybe-after-a-little-nap.' His feet felt as flat as they
were, but his stomach wasn't. His hair, though still blond,
resembled a patch in the lawn the dog had passed too often.
Smiling was something, for him, you did to air out your teeth.

He was a house on the edge of a mud slide when a drought set
in.

The Rose Café got its name from the street named Rose
Avenue which got its name from the flower which grew
profusely in the area. People came to the Rose Café like walking
scripts full of dialogue they wanted to hear themselves repeat.
They wore clothes befitting casting couches or motorcycles or
protest marches denouncing the plights of third world Latinos.
They ate animal-free dishes with French and Italian names,
drank liberated water, and sat on stools that reminded them
constantly of their bad postures. They laughed too loud and
avoided establishing eye contact with anyone at their immediate
table.

The garden was trellised with bougainvillea, as opposed to
roses, and the Rose Café veterans who had already settled their
deals for the day, or already gotten laid, or just wanted to avoid
hearing Linda Ronstadt singing in Spanish on the sound system
inside, sat out there. They were usually equipped with the *L.A.
Weekly* to plot out their plans for what not to do on the
weekend.

The golden-boy-gone-brown slid into his seat at the table next
to the fence that separated the yard from the parking lot behind.
The fence was covered with more bougainvillea but if you
craned your neck, you could see over it from a sitting position.
But he felt as much like craning as he did walking or any other
kind of physical movement, so he ignored it. He unfolded his
newspaper, took a sip of his Nicaraguan de-caf, and managed to
lift his eyebrows only slightly as the acidic flavor assaulted his
tastebuds. He crammed a piece of carrot cake into his mouth to
mask the reaction. It was down to that he thought: take one

thing to mask the reaction of another. Thirst, coffee. Coffee, cake. More thirst, more coffee, toilet. Life was a chain reaction. What philosophy said all this three thousand years ago or something. Which fuckin' Greek knew it all along only couldn't put it down in plain old English. And what fuckin' Buddha was it that said you had to live long enough to get wise enough to understand what the fuckin' Greek meant in the first place. Bullshit. It was all bullshit. Life was nothing but learning how to die so someone could find your bones and use them for a funeral pyre to bury someone else.

She felt like an old lady today but since it wasn't night, she couldn't pick any flowers from the neighbor's garden. Just a few leaves off the plant in the kitchen window which she'd rolled up into a nice little number and smoked before venturing out into the Garden-of-not-really-Eden to look for another apple to bite into. When she got to the Rose Café she plunked her piece of pecan pie down on the table which stood next to the bougainvillea plant in the centre of the café's backyard. She leaned back, looked up, and squinted into the trellised blossoms.

Could be a convention of tiny beings in O'Keeffe costumes, she imagined. Or some kind of tropical insect's cocoons. Or, Andean flute music without the sound. Or, or, or. 'Or' was her alternative form of Ohm. The right substance put in her body could keep her in a state of 'or' for hours sometimes.

The Vietnamese busboy was going from table to table collecting empty cups, plates with burnt edges of pastry left on them, and used mineral water bottles onto his trolley. As he came over to her table she smiled, not at him really, but in his direction, and he smiled back. As she registered what he was doing, she noticed the newspaper on his trolley, obviously having been discarded, which he was clearing away, and she reached over and asked him, 'May I?' The Vietnamese man smiled and nodded, gave her the newspaper and continued over to the next table.

She turned to the page with the horoscopes.

> You may be disrupted by an unexpected event. You may need to call upon your inner resources in order to cope. Don't try to distance yourself. Endeavor to be tolerant. Remember, silver can line the heart of what one sometimes sees as dark.

Hmm, she said to herself. It's gotta be a man. Isn't it always? Just hope the son of a bitch has a good stash.

At that moment she heard shouting at the other end of the garden next to the fence. The busboy was standing next to his trolley which was overturned, dishes and garbage strewn around it, and a man, who had apparently been sitting at the table, was standing, waving a newspaper in the air. The busboy started screaming, a high indecipherable stream of sounds which resembled birds attacking one another. Another employee, also Vietnamese, joined the busboy and started screaming in the bird language too. A couple at another table near the scene got up and went back inside the café.

She watched as if at the movies. Silent movies with a foreign music sound track. Now the two Vietnamese men also had newspapers and were swatting at the air. Some kind of martial art, she thought. They are practicing. Without completely standing, she edged over to the next table which was closer to the scene. Then she moved over to the next one, even closer. Finally, she was one table away. The three men continued swatting at the air. She tried to see a pattern in their movements, choreography. If they'd only do each movement simultaneously, in sync. Another employee came out of the café and joined the others. He was Mexican. He spoke to his colleagues in Spanish. He found a newspaper and started imitating the others.

Somehow, the man by the fence, still swatting, came round

the table. The other three men, also still swatting, stepped aside for him, and the man, without seeing her, moved near her table.

'I oughta fuckin' sue,' he screamed, 'I oughta call my bastard lawyer and fuckin' sue.' The rolled-up newspaper in his hand was still batting away but not so fiercely now.

Suddenly, something like tiny hot pieces of stars entered the back of her neck. The stars, upon entering the flesh, found the bloodstream and floated down it, melting into a liquid fire. Soon, she thought before passing out, soon it will be dark enough to pick those flowers.

She awoke to a bouquet of heliotrope, three gardenias with browning edges, and a half-dozen purple asters in a peanut butter jar on the table next to the bed. It was a small room and, as she looked around, she realized she was plugged into many tubes which were plugged into a battery of machines at the other side of the bed.

I have been stolen, she said.

Just then, a young nurse, too big for her uniform and with an angry spot on her left cheek near her mouth, came into the room.

'Ah,' the nurse said, 'Finally!' The nurse ran out of the room.

I have been stolen and put in a film starring Jack Nicholson she said.

The nurse re-entered the room almost immediately, followed by a man who did not look like Jack Nicholson but might have been Humphrey Bogart's father. He was followed by another nurse. They came over to her and stood close. Their faces moved. The word 'smile' came to her mind.

'How are you feeling?' the man asked.

Feeling? She lay there trying to decide what he meant.

'Pretty rough, I imagine,' the man answered his own question after a few seconds. 'You've had a long, hard struggle.' He took her arm and wrapped something black and padded around it. Then he squeezed a bulb at the end of a tube that was connected to the black padded thing and she realized she now knew what the word 'feel' meant.

'I feel squeezed,' she said.

The man's face moved again and he looked at the others and their faces moved too.

'Just checking your blood pressure,' he said. When he'd finished, he leaned closer, and with the tips of his fingers, lifted her eyelids.

Science fiction, she said to herself, I have been stolen and put into a science fiction movie where tiny beings inhabit the eyeballs of humans.

'They're still dilated a bit, but they seem to be getting clearer.' The man looked over at the battery of machines which she was plugged into. He leaned across her and flipped a switch, then sat back down on the edge of her bed. He looked at her and his face moved again only this time the word smile did not enter her mind. The word 'squint' did.

'Can you hear me OK?' he asked.

She thought about it.

'I think so,' she answered wondering if there were other things he'd said she hadn't heard.

'Can I ask you a few questions then?' he smiled and she realized it *was* a smile and not just a word.

'I think you can,' she answered, thrown by the word 'can'. The man turned to the other nurse who handed him a clipboard. He took a pen from the pocket of his white coat.

'Well, first of all, do you remember what happened?'

She heard her mind dusting itself off. Then she saw a rolladex file turning thousands of cards around in a circle until it stopped at one card. She read the card.

'Pieces of stars entered the back of my neck,' she answered.

The man smiled and looked at the nurses who also smiled.

'Well, actually, it wasn't stars.'

Her mind looked at the card again.

'It was a wasp,' the man said before she could answer. 'You

had an extreme reaction to a huge angry wasp sting. You are one of those people who is deathly allergic to their poison. You really had us going. We thought we'd lost you a few times there.'

Lost, she said to herself, not stolen.

'It seems that a man at the Rose Café was sitting next to this nest of wasps without knowing it, and a few of them discovered the carrot cake he was eating. He started swatting at them, then apparently a few employees of the restaurant joined in. The wasps came from a hole in the fence where they'd built a nest. This man punched at the nest with his newspaper which only made matters worse. At least, that's what Mr Wallbridge told us. He's the man who escorted you in the ambulance to the hospital. He explained that one of the wasps that was after him must have wandered over and stung you instead.

Mr Wallbridge? she thought.

Later that afternoon, after two cups of tea, some lemonade and the first food she'd taken in twenty-four hours, she sat up in bed and tried to discover what new things her mind was waking up to. Whatever the drugs were they'd given her – or maybe it was the wasp's poison – whichever – she now realized it had been interesting shit. She looked over at the flowers in the jar. They were blossoms just like the ones she might have picked when out on one of her night prowls. The doctor had said Mr Wallbridge had brought them. Yesterday Mr Wallbridge had left her at the hospital after he'd come with her in the ambulance, and then returned later in the afternoon with the flowers. There was no note.

The room being a typically sterile hospital room, suddenly seemed airless to her. She didn't know where this hospital was but she assumed it had to be somewhere near the beach, somewhere not too far from home. She felt her legs move until she found herself sitting on the side of the bed. Her legs continued to propel her towards the window, and she observed her hands reaching up towards the latch that seemed to

hermetically seal the room. When it wouldn't budge she forgot
to observe what she was doing and her mind entered her body's
actions as she struggled to open the window. It was as though it
had never been opened and it held fast. She stood at the window
feeling like a pressed butterfly. She wondered how she would
look pressed, eyes, nose, lips flattened like a person in a Francis
Bacon painting. She pulled a chair over to the window and stood
on it to see if she could reach the upper part of the frame and
perhaps jiggle it enough to open it. As she was reaching up and
pounding at the top of the frame she heard the door open behind
her.

'No, don't,' the man yelled with an urgency that made her
almost fall off the chair. Before she knew it, two freckled but
strong arms picked her up and carried her back to the bed and
placed her carefully down upon it as if laying out a new evening
gown to be stepped into for a ball.

'I was just . . .' she attempted to speak but realized she had
forgotten why she was just. Just was never a word she used to
apply to herself. She looked up at the man who resembled
someone who needed rescuing rather than someone who was a
rescuer. The freckled arms led up to a short-sleeved Hawaiian
flowered shirt exposing a tuft of gold-going-gray hair at the top
of the chest. He wore a Swatch on his left wrist. Her eyes felt like
a periscope prying up through miles of water to inspect enemy
territory, only to find that the natives were friendly.

'I don't think you should be moving around too much yet,' he
said. His face was a leather bag on which two robin's eggs lay. He
wasn't smiling but as his lips moved she saw lines appear in his
cheeks as if old dimples had been elongated by gravity. 'You
never know with these goddamn things.'

'You must be Mr . . .'

'Wallbridge. Ivan Wallbridge.' He pushed his hands in the
pockets of his jeans to keep himself from thrusting one out at
her to suggest a handshake.

'You're the one with the flowers.' She wanted to look at those hands. So far, those hands had swatted air that turned out to be wasps, picked flowers from other people's gardens and carried her from the chair to the bed. They were obviously objects of diverse talents.

'From my garden,' he answered. 'Or rather, my landlady's garden.' He looked over at the battery of monitors and equipment she was no longer hooked up to. 'You must be getting better. At least you don't have all that stuff wired up to you anymore.'

'Yeah, but I'm still wired, if you know what I mean.' She couldn't honestly say she knew what she meant. With her words she saw his eyes light up as though he might smile but his lips managed to stifle it.

He nodded his head in understanding. 'Good stuff, hospital drugs,' he responded.

'Yeah, I guess. Except there's no place to go to enjoy them, if you know what I mean. Just this boring room. The window won't even open so you can breathe.' She watched as he took his hands out of his pockets and went over to the window. He knocked at the frame in four places, then simply opened it. A warm breeze filtered into the room.

'Ah, smog,' she said, thanks ringing the tone of her voice. 'Nothing like the smell of L.A.'

'Humph,' he grunted, putting his hands back into his pockets and returning to her bedside. He looked around. 'I think you ought to get out of this place as soon as possible. Places like this make your skin peel.'

She suddenly felt herself itching. What started as a little itch spread rapidly from the tips of her toes up to her scalp. She started scratching. She scratched her leg, then her arm, her breast, her cheek.

'I'm sorry,' he said anxiously as he realized what she was doing. 'Those drugs must have made you suggestible.' He left the room and by the time he returned with a nurse, she was scratching so furiously her arms and legs were blotched and red.

'It's a reaction,' the nurse said, filling a hypodermic with something from a tube of liquid. 'To the poison I suspect.' The nurse turned her on her side and the needle pricked her buttock.

'Or the drugs,' he said sourly, folding his arms across the flowers on his shirt. The nurse didn't look at him but raised her eyes up in her head.

'You'll feel better in just a few minutes,' she said. 'And the doctor has said you can be released late this afternoon. He'll be in to check on you before you leave.'

She rolled over on her back again and watched as Ivan followed the nurse to the door. As the nurse left, he turned to her.

'Do you have a way home? I mean, do you have anybody to pick you up?' She thought of him picking her up as she had stood on the chair at the window.

'You,' she answered. 'I have you to pick me up.'

Showing no surprise, he nodded.

'Later,' he said, closing the door behind him.

Ivan's vw bus shifted into fourth upon entering the Santa Monica freeway. She was used to vw buses. She'd known about as many vw buses as she had the men who usually drove them. It takes a certain kind of person to own a vw bus, she'd decided. At least it took a certain kind of person to own one for about fifteen years which was how long most of the men owned the buses she had ridden in. And this one was no exception. If Ivan hadn't owned this vw for at least fifteen years she'd be mightily surprised.

Ivan had strapped her into the passenger's seat using two old belts. He said the original seatbelt had broken a long time ago so he used belts instead. He'd asked her if she'd rather lie down in the rear of the bus. The middle seat had been taken out so there was a wide gap between the front and the back seat which was cluttered with rusty tools, beer cans and a cardboard box full of paperbacks.

Though it was past rush hour, the traffic on the freeway was still heavy and they stopped and started, spurting their way west towards the beach.

'You doing OK?' he asked at one of the stops.

Her mind no longer consulted its private rolladex file like it had when she'd first regained consciousness in the hospital. It moved like a sheet of ice that had been dislodged from a defrosting freezer and thrown into the kitchen sink. Or like the left-over maple syrup on the three bites of pancakes you couldn't quite finish eating. Or like the clothes hanging out on the line in a rain storm. She was back to her 'ors' once again. She must be getting well.

Well, she thought.

'I said, you doing OK, Angelica?' His voice was ringed with alarm at her non-answer.

'Well,' she answered.

'Well?' His face crinkled in a question mark.

'I'm getting well,' she stated. The realization that she was getting better had come slowly and only now, in what seemed to be hours since she'd replied did it dawn upon her that he'd said her name.

'You're a clairvoyant, right?' she said. She tried to figure out where the word 'clairvoyant' had come from in her head.

'What?'

'You know my name,' she answered, still amazed that her tongue was carrying on this verbal interaction.

'Oh.' He almost smiled but caught himself. 'I had to look in your handbag for an ID. You know, yesterday, for the hospital. That's also how I know where you live, now that I'm taking you home.'

'Then you know the rest?'

'The rest?' He frowned, something he was good at.

'Of my name.'

'Oh.' He looked at her, then back at the traffic, then back at her again. 'Yeah, but do you?'

Her face was empty. 'I think it has something to do with the beach,' she said.

'Wow,' he said, shifting again and exiting the freeway. He pulled over to the side of the street and parked, not turning off the ignition. 'You're still wading in it pretty thick, aren't you?'

She looked at him and then at her feet to see what she could possibly be wading in.

'Sands,' he said. 'Your name is Angelica Sands.'

'Ah, *that's* right.' She laid her head back against the seat and closed her eyes. 'I think I hear them,' she said.

'Hear what?'

'Those angels my mother said would always be with me 'cause of my name. They're brushing sand off their wings. Been a long flight. Whoosh. Whoosh. Whoosh.'

She woke up to the smell of coffee. It was a shiny smell and made her feel polished, clean. She was lying on her own bed in her own little one-room apartment. The windows were all open. She heard the rustling of newspapers in the kitchen.

'Do they call you Ives?' she said loud enough to be heard in the kitchen. The newspaper crumpled loudly. Quick footsteps rustled towards her.

'You OK?' he asked, standing by her bed.

'I'm ... yes.' Her ability to actually think was returning.

'I called the hospital when we got here. You passed out again, in the car you know. Anyway, I called them and they said you were probably still having this reaction, so I just needed to put you to bed and keep a close watch. They phoned in a script.' He went back into the kitchen and returned with a bottle of pills. 'You gotta take one of these four times a day till they're finished.' He handed them to her.

'Do they?' she asked.

'What?' His hands scratched at his hair.

'Call you Ives?'

He looked at her and sat on the edge of her bed, then reached over and touched her forehead as if to check for fever. When assured she had none, he leaned back and looked at her.

'Well, first of all, there is no "they", and second of all, no.' She thought she saw a bit of a smile, but the room was dark except for the light from the kitchen, so she couldn't be sure. 'But you can call me that I guess, if you want to.' He turned in profile to her and she saw his lips mouth the word 'Ives'.

'Sorta like Charles?' she suggested.

'What?' he turned to her again, his face screwed up in total confusion.

'Sorta like Charles Ives, the composer who wrote all that weird music.'

He stood and pulled up his jeans, looked at her, went into the kitchen and returned with two cups of coffee.

'Tell me something,' he said as he returned to the kitchen to get some sugar. 'Is it the drugs, the poison or,' he came back in, 'or does your mind always work like this?'

They're on the beach, only not Santa Monica beach, but up north, near Point Reyes. It's cold and they both have on down jackets. Sandpipers chase each other along the water line. The waves come in looking angry and powerful, and even though it's only mid-afternoon the sun looks tired as if it's thinking of getting to bed early to get a good night's sleep.

They walk with their hands in their pockets. She bends over every now and then, picks up a shell, looks at it and either pockets it or throws it back on the beach. He's telling her about the last ten years of his life. They've been together now long enough for him to have already told her about the first thirty-five.

She listens as though she is holding a glass to her ear, as though there's a wall between his room and hers. As though she needs to clean the wax out of her ears. She can't believe he has so little of significance to report, so she thinks if she can only hear better, maybe there will be more. They sit on a long tree branch

someone has dragged out to the beach to be used as a seat. She's
already told him she can't remember much of her own life but
that it doesn't matter. She told him this right after he'd told her
about his first sixteen years, hoping he'd take the hint, which he
hadn't. He seemed to be a tipped pitcher full of memories
pouring out on to her. It was OK though. Somewhere along the
way, San Luis Obispo she thought it was, she had remembered
the horoscope from the newspaper at the Rose Café. 'Endeavor
to be tolerant' was about all she could remember from it. Her
mind, though still its usual free-form self, was getting back its
strength, and each day the relationship between it and her body
seemed more compatible.

That first night, after he'd asked her about how her mind
worked, they'd begun to talk like they were in a contest. Like
there was a murderer waiting outside to kill them if they
stopped. Like they'd scored some first-rate crystal meth. Of
course, he'd done most of the narrative talking because her
words usually came out condensed in little packages like Zen
koans without the Master. But it had been as if they were
darning the holes in each other's only pair of socks, and now he
had one of hers and one of his on, and she had on one of his and
one of her own.

'So Barbara,' he continues his narrative about his ex-wife,
'She kept saying it was because I fell on that rock pile and hit my
head on that hard rock when I was six. She said that I could
never get it together because there was something wrong with
me because of that.'

'Your head seems OK to me,' she said.

He actually smiled at her and chucked at her chin. He had
finally started smiling the night they started talking. 'That's just
'cause I'm new to you, that's all. When I get old to you you'll
change your view on that.' He looked out at the gray waves.

She thought about what he'd said.

'Things never get old to me,' she answered. 'They just
disappear before they get old.' She thought of her sound system

that got stolen when she'd had it for three years. She thought of the marijuana in the pot in the kitchen window that never got properly harvested because she always clipped its leaves before it grew into maturity. She thought of her parents who'd died young.

They walked over to the cliff that jutted up dramatically from the beach. Fingers of boulders reached out across the beach and into the water. They started climbing the boulders and finally perched on one and looked out at the water.

'You from L.A.? I mean, originally?' he asked as he picked up a stone, looked at it, threw it towards the ocean, picked up another one.

'Nah,' she answered and found herself imitating him in picking up stones. 'Chama.'

'Chama? Where's that!'

'New Mexico. Chama, New Mexico.' The expression on his face asked how, why, when. 'I hitchhiked. 1970. Caught a ride with a logger down to Abiquiui, then another one to Albuquerque, then another one to Flagstaff, then one all the way to Bakersfield. Took me six months to get outta Bakersfield and make it to the beach. Been here ever since.' She picked up a piece of another rock. 'Hey, look at this.' The rock was sliced in half, and upon examination there appeared to be a tiny fossil embedded in it.

'What do they call these things?' she asked as she showed it to him. He turned it over and studied it carefully.

'Some kind of fossil,' he answered, putting his whole palm around it. She reached over and put her hand on his and he opened his palm. She pulled his hand which held the rock over to her lap and cupped it in her hands. She looked down at the rock again.

'I found a fossil once in New Mexico. There was this old guy at the gas station I showed it to. He used to work for an oil company and he knew some things about rocks and stuff. I showed it to him and he said it was called a trilobite. That's what he said the fossil was, a trilobite. It was funny looking. He said those animals don't live anymore. They're extinct.' She clasped his hand with the rock in it tightly in her hands.

'Sorta like what we'll all be when the rest of us are as old as this is,' he said, meaning the fossil.

'You mean extinct?'

'Yeah.'

She thought about it. 'You mean if an ice age or a volcano or something comes along and traps us in a rock?'

'Yeah,' he smiled.

'And then what's left of us is discovered millions of years from now by something that actually discovers things?'

'Yeah.'

'What if we're the only ones?'

'You mean the only discovered remnants of human beings?' he asks.

'Yeah, and they've got nothing to compare us with.'

'Hmm.'

'And if they have nothing left to compare us with, then they won't know what human beings are really supposed to be like, will they?'

'Well, I guess . . .'

'So if they don't know how people are supposed to really be then we could fool them, couldn't we?'

'Well . . .'

She took the rock from his hand and laid it carefully on a boulder at her side, then took off her down jacket, laid it on the boulder and put the rock on it. Then she moved over to him and began taking off his down jacket. He went along with her, caught up in what seemed like some kind of destiny. She laid his jacket down on a large boulder behind her and began undressing. As he watched her, his hands automatically started unbuttoning the buttons of his shirt.

They slid into each other like the stars into the sky. Stars that had been there all along. They'd been there all along but the light had obscured the fact. Angelica and Ives' bodies had belonged together all along. It was just that life had obscured the fact.

'It can come now,' she said.

'What?' he murmured close in her ear.

'The ice age or the volcano or whatever it is,' she said. 'We'll fool them. We'll fool them after all.'

Drydocking in Silver Lake

The telephone rang like the devil himself. After a moment of deliberation as to whether or not she really should answer it, whether picking up the receiver would banish her forever from the garden of what she really had to do, she succumbed and finally picked it up. It was Andy, of course, with more questions about files and names. These were things he needed to know to be able to take over her position at the newspaper, so she had to be patient with him. Two weeks, and he still called three or four times a day with a 'Who is Anne Dunlap and why are there three stars by her name?' Or, 'When did you last have contact with Juan Romero?'

The pattern of the last few weeks had gone like this: After Andy's call, a little later in the morning, there would be the call from Frankie complaining about Ted Rosen's latest rough draft. Then Jennie would call to report on what bitchy thing some actor had said about some director who'd crashed a party the night before after a preview. Eventually, around four o'clock, Antonia would be on the other end, sucking her nicotine gum, and entering into her half-hour monologue about why George, her ex-husband, had screwed up her chances of ever having a healthy relationship again.

It seemed like her world had gotten to the point where everybody sucked off everybody else; there were psychological tubes slowly dripping from the psyches of everyone she knew into the back of her head. But her own tube had backed up, a glob of desire for experiencing something more meaningful blocking it from dripping over to them. She was beginning to feel like a ship that needed drydocking to have all its barnacles or whatever scraped off. Then she'd move smoothly out to that sea she'd been waiting so long to sail.

She knew she had to do her own drydocking. Discipline was another word for it. Schedule. Rhythm. Equilibrium. After all, there was now no need to be gallivanting around L.A. in the Isuzu Trooper, off to the next press conference. There was no next meeting to determine the next story that might be developed. No next country to be assigned to for a series of reports on how the next coup was going. No more next foreign film festival, next Washington scandal. No more next any-things. Journalistically anyway. That string of nexts that had hung around her neck for fifteen years had finally been broken when she'd stormed into Warren's office and demanded a year's severance pay. If there had been one thing she'd learned from all those years of playing hard ball with the big boys, it was slam it down tough. So she had, and had fired it straight past the hitter into the glove of her imagined destiny, and one week later the check was in her hands and she had walked out of the newspaper office for the last time.

She semi-deflated as she snuggled back down under her covers and looked around her bedroom. For one week solid she'd been boxing up the stacks of papers and books, the clippings, notes, files. Seventeen boxes hauled down to the garage so far. Her Isuzu, now parked on the street, was unable to fit into the garage any longer. She thought of all those paths in her apartment she'd created over the years to get through the accumulated mountains of boxes and stacks of papers and books, her collected 'research' materials. Tools of the trade. Over the last days those paths from the bedroom to the bathroom to the kitchen to the living room, had widened further and further until she was now down to three large stacks of papers and files and was confronted with actual rooms to be moved around in rather than paths. Now she could actually get out of bed and walk to the bathroom from more than one direction. She did so and, upon entering it, she took pleasure in remembering that she'd even ravaged the bathroom. She was now down to her hairbrush, her toothbrush, the toothpaste, the Paul Mitchell shampoo, the awapuhi conditioner, the blow drier, the carrot moisturizer, a wand of mascara, the tube of Erase and the bottle of Advil. If she kept on like this her life would become simple as corn rows with nothing round the roots except good red dirt.

Speaking of red, she assessed her hair. One of her trade-marks. Its tangles now fell in unflattering angles around her face and threatened mouse brown. It reminded her of some kind of herbal toothpaste, like the one she'd gotten rid of in her recent purge. Her face looked pasty too as if she lived in England or had a sun allergy that required her always to wear hats. The peaches and cream of yesteryear had over-ripened and gone to cheese, and the wrinkles! Who would have ever thought that the law of gravity would be a lesson only truly learned when the face started to prove it? Right now, as she looked into the bathroom mirror, she could think only of her Uncle Homer's bloodhound. The eyes themselves, which had always defied the label of any one color but were closer to green than anything, now struck her as something kin to a weimaraner dog, pale and lost in the scramble of the rest of her face.

'Sugar,' she said to herself. 'You went to shit and the hogs ate it.' She shook her head at herself and splashed her face, rubbed some carrot moisturizer on it, yanked a brush through her tangles, and commanded herself to the kitchen. Eating her bowl of European muesli, she stared out the kitchen window, down on the scene she'd taken for granted for so long: The Silver Lake District, its funky hills smattered with the occasional Spanish red-tiled roof, its mixture of billboards in English and Spanish, its century plants and iceplant and old transplanted palm trees.

Coyotes still came down here, after the rats that hid in the foliage. She never watched for them anymore. A helicopter made its way across her vision. Highway reporter, she assumed without wondering; the ones at night with their macho spotlights were the cops but, during the day, it was the highway guys or else some private number headed for Century City. In the old days, no 'copters, no Spanish billboards, no Thais at the laundromat or Cambodians in the back busing dishes in the kitchen of the nouvelle cuisine bistro. No nouvelle cuisine bistro.

She poured herself a cup of Earl Grey and took it into the living room. Two weeks now. In two weeks she'd backed her rising time from twelve o'clock up to ten-thirty up to nine-thirty and now eight-thirty. Each new shift in time presented her with a different view from the windows, different people going different places in different amounts of traffic under a different angle of the sun. That first week she answered the phone then went back to sleep. By the second week she made herself rise after the third phone call, then the second, and by now she was managing to get up after the first call of the day. Just right. Luckily she now thought she knew no human being on the face of the earth who would call her before eight-thirty in the morning. Except, of course, Beth, in Singapore, who never knew *when* she was calling because of the time difference. Or occasionally Jimmy who'd ring her from Managua whenever he could manage to get a hold of a phone.

'Ah, Jimmy. Now that could have . . .' she caught herself from saying it to herself. She'd long ago quit saying such things to herself. Jimmy was Jimmy. Jimmy was *gone* is what Jimmy was. Jimmy was *always* gone as far as that went. He'd been going since she'd first met him in Honduras, him down there for the *Times*, her for her newspaper.

'And Fidel . . .' she added to herself as if thinking of another man was the only possible way to distract her from thinking about Jimmy. Of course Fidel's real name was Aaron but she'd gone back and forth between calling him Fidel and Fido the whole time they'd been in Havana together covering the film festival there in ... '85 was it? Well, anyway, good ol' Fidel/ Fido/Aaron had had a real tail between his legs.

She allowed herself a few moments of wallowing in the yesteryear, then rose from her rocking chair ... the one Stephen had left behind in 1978 because he couldn't get it into his VW and couldn't bear ever to see her again ... and went back into the bedroom, slipped on her khakis, changed the red football jersey she slept in for the burnt orange tunic with the three-quarter length sleeves, and shuffled over to the Smith Corona. The list sat beside the typewriter. It was the one thing she'd written so far, the list, but you had to start somewhere. She read it over once again:

> Greek worry beads around the neck of a dead body in
> San Salvador.
> The watch on Ida Lupino's wrist as she sat thinking.
> Jasmine wreaths piled on the fresh roadside grave in
> Guatemala.
> The crinkle in the corner of Duvall's mouth when he
> sat thinking.
> Mounds of dead fish on the beach in Nicaragua.
> Didion's geraniums on the terrace where she sat
> staring out to sea.
> Five milagros left behind in the room in Las Islas
> in Mexico City.

So far, it was as far as she'd got with her marvelous new writing career.

So, the gangs were at it again. This time three guys stabbed on Washington Avenue at ten forty-five the night before. Five men arrested. None of them had done it, of course, she figured, as she finished reading the morning paper. They never got the real baddies but always came up with someone to blame it on to make it look like they were doing their jobs being the great ol' movie-star-macho-pig-cops the LAPD had always prided themselves in being.

Because she'd actually woken at eight o'clock this morning . . . Andy had called, madder than a wet hen, desperate for advice on how to handle Marguerite (Warren's secretary) . . . she'd allowed herself the extra half hour to read the morning paper. Not a habit she wanted to get into, she reminded herself. Same old shit anyway.

The day before she'd added to her list:

> Where Imelda Marcos's three pairs of shoes have gone since they were stolen from her thousands of pairs during the palace take-over.

> John Major's observations about the homeless of London while under the influence of ecstasy being dropped into his morning coffee at regular intervals for three weeks.

> A Baptist couple from Texas in their seventies are sedated and flown to Sudan where they wake up to stars in the desert.

By then Antonia had called, begging her to go to lunch. She was in desperate straits, convinced that George had spiked her recent prescription of nicotine gum with speed because she hadn't slept for three nights. The two hour lunch at the Rose Café, ending in Carlos showing up and demanding to take her to watch the sunset on Venice Beach, had put an end to her work for the day. It was true she hadn't watched a sunset in probably three years. And it was also true that Carlos needed her to listen to his dilemma; his lover, Charles, had tested positive. She and Carlos had downed three tequila sunrises and a cup of Hawaiian de-caf at the Shack before she'd rolled herself home feeling like a dethorned cactus full of sap.

'No more of that, my lordess, no more of that,' she scolded herself. 'It's the ol' shit-or-get-off-the-pot time.' She was beginning to think she was going to have to split the scene. Disconnect. Vacate. Unoccupy. Grow her nails and dig them into the flesh of her life. Amputate, dissect, perform surgery on her relationships. Somehow she just *knew* that if she went on like this her shadow would get longer and longer filling up all the space around her until it took her over completely. She was becoming an L.A. country and western song with all the words to all the tunes punchable on the jukebox of life by any finger that knew her number. My God, she thought, I am beginning to feel like a character Diane Keaton would've played in the seventies.

The telephone rang. She let it. She watched the thing, thinking she could almost see it thrashing about like in a cartoon. Its face stuck its tongue out at her. With a movement she thought of as rather balletic actually, she unplugged it from the wall. Thanks, but no thanks, sweetie. That done, and in one continuous action, she moved into the bedroom, picked up the sheet of paper and plunged it into the typewriter:

What the six foot tall redheaded woman does after she cuts her hair into a Jean Seberg, makes tea from it mixed with senna, drinks it, shits for twenty-four hours, sells all her possessions, gives up her apartment, gives her Isuzu to Carlos, makes five phone calls and splits for England.

She couldn't think of anything else to add; it seemed quite complete. She got up from the typewriter. Turned on the tea kettle in the kitchen, took the senna out of the cupboard and put it on the counter, found her scissors in the knife drawer and headed to the bathroom.

The tea kettle started singing. In the bathroom the scissors clicked.

What was it Beatrice had to say?

She was bordering on self-pity so she ordered herself to the kitchen, foraged the fridge, discovered last night's leftovers and, as she stood there cramming cold noodles with pesto sauce down her gullet, she started scribbling a list:

Profiteroles
The Twin Peaks cassette tape
Japanese fan with crane
Freesia

That done, she tore the sheet of paper from the pad and started another one:

The man at the airport who looked like Tolstoy.
Shedding jacarandas next to a pond in Durban.
The wild horse in the woods near Perugia.
The cockney medium speaking fluent Chinese while in
     a trance.
Pillows stuffed with hair.

Yes, she thought to herself as she read over the last list, these were all strong images to work with. Bound to be good for a poem or a story or something. And, as for the first list, Alfredo *did* make the greatest profiteroles she'd ever tasted. Those kind

131

that make you think you've never tasted any of the ingredients ever before in anything else. Now, if she had a dozen of them, say, some Amaretto, the Twin Peaks tape playing sexily and mysteriously in the background, the Japanese fan open on the mantelpiece with the blue glass vase full of freesia in front of it, the right man would have to . . .

She kept herself from saying it.

At this point in her life, 'Falling into love' sounded like a form of medieval punishment, or a childhood superstition or some kind of accident like stepping in dog shit in the middle of the night.

What she really wanted was for this experience, this event to be what it was supposed to be: she wanted it to seem like one of life's great occurrences such as viewing a first sunset over the Pacific, or waking up in a city where no one speaks your language, or looking up and seeing migrating parrots mating in mid-flight. She wanted to shake up her phantom lover's senses and fill them with who she was. That accomplished, she would then leave him. Exit while he was still in that altered state of being that made it seem like he could not live without her.

She owed it to him. The right man. She owed him that at least. She figured she owed a lot to a lot of men. *All* the right men. They had, after all, made her who she was: prematurely gray and hungry. Floundering about with a bloated mind and anorexic heart.

If she ever found any more right men, she must remember to try to do this. Leave them. Wanting more.

No, that wasn't right, she corrected herself. That was a remnant of her vengeful thirties speaking, the age of Blame-It-All-On-Someone-Else. This was her mature forties now, the enlightened, forgiving, Take-Responsibility-For-Your-Own-Actions period of life.

'A little relapse into the ol' victim mode, my dear,' she said to herself, shaking her finger at her image in the kitchen mirror. The mirror was in a frame that was decorated with mushrooms and carrots and asparagus. Cute. Tiffany, her flat-mate had a mirror in every room of the flat. Luckily, all of them did not have vegetables on them.

She walked through the sitting room as she headed back to her own room. Tiffany's sitting room, she thought. Tiffany's flat. She actually *lived* with someone called Tiffany. She'd moved in six months before when Tiffany, an American airline stewardess stationed in London, placed an ad in *Time Out* for someone to share her flat. Anything would be better than the place she'd had before, she'd told herself when Tiffany had first shown her around the flat. She'd refused to let herself pass judgement on Tiffany's taste in furniture and decoration, a taste that unfortunately lived up to her eventual flat-mate's name. But after six months of living here, her previous tolerance had conceded defeat to her dominating judgemental side, and she now found herself almost nauseated every time she walked through the front door. This was not a liberated way to think, she scolded herself. But her nose crinkled as she walked through the sitting room and caught sight of Tiffany's collection of toads which sat on the driftwood-base and glass-topped coffee table.

She sighed as she sat back on her bed, and opened her black book to jot down a line that blinked in her brain like a neon sign. Lately, there had been a lot of neon signs, a veritable Las Vegas strip, blaring away, using too much electricity, stripping her of her energy. If she wrote them down sometimes they became poems, and she could drop them in the mail to Jimmy in L.A. like a form of letter bringing him up to date on her life in London.

Her life. Was it so different from her life of before?

Yes it is, sugar, she conceded to her own mirror which hung on the wall opposite her bed. Maybe, after all, it was just age setting in, age with its big shoes with treads like truck tyres walking all over your body and face. No, she concluded, not just age, though of course that was a variable. But, no, her life was definitely different now and, no matter how she looked at it, she had the feeling that it had been altered permanently. Her life would be different from here on out, regardless of where she lived or what she did because she had come here. To England. To this flat. To this place in her life. She had known it was going to be before she had done it. Back home in California, she had quit her job on the newspaper and she had sold her furniture. She had packed her bags and, taking many deep breaths, written her goodbye letter to Jimmy who had been away at the time, covering a story in Honduras. The letter had been a masterpiece ... she hoped he would save it always in case someone ever wanted to put together her collected letters ... but, upon his return, it had taken him five days before he had even opened it. She knew this because he had contacted one of their mutual friends when he'd eventually gotten around to thinking about her and wondered where the hell she was.

So, her accumulated savings in hand, she had headed out for the future. To experience. To live. To get over Jimmy. To get over all the others. But had her life, the essence of her, really changed?

Oh, honey!

She sat there, black book on lap, and looked around her room. All that was left of her forty-five years of accumulated possessions was squeezed into this room. She lived with an ageing flower child cum airline stewardess named Tiffany. The men she now met all seemed like they were auditioning for some play in which she was the understudy to the leading lady. They either got the part and moved on to make it with the star somewhere else out there, or they didn't return for call-backs.

Ah, honey, you got washed up on a desert island and there were just a few teeny little things which might have made it all a little easier to deal with. She made another list.

Flour tortillas
A good friend who has seen as many movies as I have
Jimmy

There you go again, she said to herself. Always having to include a man . . . him especially . . . in some recipe for contentment. She tore the page out of her black book, wadded it up and threw it at the waste paper basket. Missed.

WHAT AM I PLAYING AT she wrote in big black letters on a clean white page of her book. The big ball game of life? What a sport. She was getting too old to play this game and yet she continued. One more season. The games getting shorter each time. Pop fouls. Left field.

Never could even find a uniform that fit, she said out loud to the closet that held her clothes as she pulled down a green shirt and put it on over the peach t-shirt. 'I should retire to coaching,' she said. Then she stopped and thought about it. 'I *have* retired to coaching,' she answered herself, thinking about the string of younger men she'd been seeing over the year since she'd been here. 'They come up from the farm teams to the Big Leagues, I coach 'em for a while, and then they go hit 'em out of the park.' She slammed the door to her closet, threw her keys into her bag, and closed the door to the flat behind her as fast as she could.

It was not any better out on the street. Although it was a beautiful street full of gorgeous houses, it was full of all the wrong people. She took the tube, changed, took another one and found herself in Covent Garden. She wandered over to the cappuccino bar, ensconced herself at a corner table, and ordered an Amaretto.

By five she'd found a player. A little short maybe but well-built. Italian. He would have no sense of the oriental aesthetic, she reminded herself, mentally striking the Japanese fan off the earlier list she'd made. And he'd probably be bored with profiteroles, even Alfredo's.

'We'll have to discover Indian together, she thought. I'll expose him to chapatis and pull out my pink sari. He'll eventually show up with saffron incense, I'll bring out the ol' Ravi Shankar and . . .

She was mentally already into the third inning by the time they left the café. Before leaving she went into the Ladies and made a quick list:

> After all, this *is* experience.
> Anyway, I've always wanted to know about Italy.
> Did Germaine Greer know what she was talking about when she said Italian men were the best?
> Do you have to love opera to appreciate the Italian mind?
> Did Romans give ibex trees their name?
> What was it Beatrice had to say about it all during her descent into hell?

Chocolate cake

I guess you could say I came along 'cause he was this white macho artist who hit a phase when he just gotta have black ... and there was my ma ... ebony shinin' at him like some kind of forbidden fruit ... so here I am.

It was way before Afros but she didn't have plaits or corn rows, just cut it short like a man which was kinda unusual for those times. When you look at her picture now ... the one with her on the swing hanging from the sycamore in Aunt Ruby's backyard ... all you see's eyes and a white sundress. Like some kind of owl. She's young then, just found out about me inside her and has nothin' to smile about. She's short too, like a girl, only never got bigger. A little ol' owl.

So here I came. She'd stopped takin' art lessons by then and started takin' tiny stitches to pink cotton cloth, making little sacks for me to wear. I came along with red hair and long bones when she had me ... always long legs, long arms ... comin' from that little bird. She drew some pictures of me I can remember .. me bendin' over waterin' some squash with my green bucket ... me sittin' on the brick edge of the front porch steps, lookin' at ants walkin' in through the front door. She stopped drawin' though when she went back to night school to be a lawyer. Guess she didn't have time enough with having to go to college and work ... she taught kindergarten ... and take care of me all at the same time. Of course Aunt Ruby helped. She was my great-aunt really, Mama's aunt. We lived with her and she'd take care of me when Mama had to work or go to school. In fact, I can't remember Mama drawing at all; I just remember Mama tired.

But much later when I guess she thought I was big enough, when she saw me coloring pictures or something one day, she sat me down. She picked some sunflowers and black-eyed Susans, put them in a jar, put it all on the backyard wall between Aunt Ruby's house and Mildred Brown's next door, and went inside for something. She came out with her old box of pencils, about six or seven of them in all numbers, and gave them to me.

She said, 'You like to try and see if you can draw these maybe?' I shrugged my shoulders and smiled like I was ready for anything. She stood there, a curious look on her face like she was thinking all sorts of mysterious things and walked away from where she'd been standing next to the flowers.

'I just want to say one thing though. Now, listen to me. Don't draw what you think you see, draw what is there, OK?' and she went inside and left me alone. I didn't know *what* to think about that.

Of course, for a while I just played with how dark the marks were for all the pencils, how skinny, how thick. From the beginning I liked the ones that drew the thickest and heaviest. But, as I kept drawin', I thought a lot about what she'd said, 'Don't draw what you think you see, draw what is there.' I figured she meant don't make anything up, not even one line, not even a dot.

She didn't say much at all for a long time about what I put down, just let me go at it and sneaked a peek every now and then. One day she came home from teachin' at Long's Elementary with these colored pencils. Let's see, there must've been about ten of them if I remember correctly: red, pink, orange, blue, green, purple, yellow, another light blue and a chartreuse and a brown. She says, 'These are for you to play with.' She saw my eyes light up. Then she said, 'Play, but, darling,' she added, 'play serious.'

138

After a couple of weeks of messin' around I entered what you might call my 'tropical stage'. This is the one where every picture has a palm tree and sand somewhere. I wasn't looking at anything then ... no real palm tree or real sand ... just pictures behind my eyes. Some had the sea. One had a girl in a grass skirt, a brown girl in a yellow grass skirt. I learned not to press down too hard and break the point but I colored that girl and her skirt so heavy the paper almost tore. Then there was the one of a new moon and a star like a magic picture I'd seen once somewhere which I colored heavy blue and got one of my regular pencils and went over it lightly then licked my fingers to smudge it in. The ones with orange and yellow and pink and green I started drawin' black around to make the thing, the object, the color stand out. To make it clearer and organized and separate from the sky or sand or sea that just went on and on and you couldn't do anything about it.

One day she says, 'Rae, you're doin' primitive!' and she took out these books and magazines full of pictures of folk art from all over the world that she'd had left over from when she knew my daddy and had drawn things herself. Oranges and greens and palm trees for sure and a lot with black lines all around. She said, 'Rae, now look.' She sat me down in Aunt Ruby's rocker and she went over to a row of bookshelves and turned to me. 'See these?' she pointed to the books. 'These are not just books, they're special ... like food ... not to eat with your mouth but with your eyes and your head. You have to learn to eat this stuff just like a baby has to learn to eat solid food when it gets big enough not just to have milk.'

I thought a lot about that for years, you know, about pictures being just like food. Some foods you just can't stand like spinach and beets, and others you'd kill for like Aunt Ruby's vanilla pudding and her chocolate cake. Some pictures you look at are like leftover creamed spinach and others are like cake so full of chocolate your eyes can taste it. Then you think eventually, well maybe I should eat some of that creamed stuff 'cause it's good for me ... makes the chocolate cake taste that much better ... so you draw things soft and pictures of pale light and wiggly lines like worms instead of stretched out snakes lying in the sun. One thing I'd say is you gotta eat your spinach before you get your chocolate cake.

So, that's it ... that's how I began to sprout inside while my outside sprouted even more, like a plant not getting enough sun ... long and gangly and paler than my ma or Aunt Ruby or any of the others in our family. Ma continued to teach at Long's and go nights to law school. Aunt Ruby continued workin' at the Gracies' being what she called a 'mammy' like her mother did before her. The Gracies lived in a big house on the white side of town and Aunt Ruby would go up there every mornin' and come back home after their supper. She'd bake them her chocolate cakes, clean and polish all their grandchildren's pictures in silver frames that sat on their grand piano. She'd come home at the end of the day sometimes, put her feet up on the footstool in front of her rocker and say, 'Whew, Mr Gracie, he's gonna have troubles he don't know the names of with those three.' She didn't much like the Gracie grandkids. They were all the time buggin' her for her chocolate cake and leavin' brown finger prints all over things.

My hair was still red ... that kind that looks like rosehips tea ... and my eyes as amber as one of those German dogs rich people have, and I was already six inches taller than Ma when I was twelve and kept going. Mister Gracie saw me once when I'd gone over to his house to give Aunt Ruby some eggs she'd asked me to bring her, and he said, 'Too bad she's not a boy, Ruby, she'd make a good basketball player', and I thought, basketball player, hell! He want a basketball player let him go find some freak white boy. He want a drawer, here I am!

My ma had graduation from Texas Southern two weeks after Aunt Ruby's funeral. Funny how good things come along at the same time as bad sometimes. Anyway, what that meant was we had just planted all the potted plants and flowers that people

had brought for Aunt Ruby's funeral, then we got more flowers
inside the house that people brought to congratulate Ma on her
graduation. Loads of flowers everywhere. Mostly yellow chrysanthemums but there was this group of hydrangeas that Mrs
Gracie brought that were different. They were the kind of blue
that's almost purple because of the soil they're put in and each
flower was like its own bouquet. Well, it was more than I could
stand; I was mesmerized. It took me days to get that color right
and when I did, you saw purple-blue dresses and purple-blue
skies and purple-blue oceans and purple-blue eyes. Picasso had
his blue period, so I guess you'd say this was my purple-blue
one. It helped me, findin' that color in those flowers. It was
how my heart felt every time I thought of Aunt Ruby's bein'
gone.

So Mama became a lawyer. First black woman lawyer in the
southern part of Texas, at least, maybe even Louisiana. Don't
know. Don't know those statistics except I was so proud of her I
felt like I had medals pinned all over me. I was sixteen by then
and ready to stop growin' but my body didn' know it. I
remember walkin' into the living room of Aunt Ruby's house
with Ma after the graduation ceremonies. She was holding her
diploma all wrapped in tissue paper, and she unwrapped it, took
it out and put it next to Aunt Ruby's picture on the mantel.
Then she came over to me and stood back lookin' at it and said,
'That's for her, you know.' We just stood there huggin' and
cryin' and wantin' some of her chocolate cake and laughin'
'cause we knew she'd be lookin' down from heaven sayin',
'That's all you loved me for, my chocolate cake.'

Which is how that series of paintings came about all those
years later . . . the ones with dark brown shiny parts that glisten
and make you wonder why you wanta eat somethin'. And how
those purple-blues finagled their way onto those canvases that
make you think I've been lookin' at a lot of Monets. I could trace
those yellows I do back to a particular picnic we had when it was
101 degrees and we'd had no rain for three months and Ma said,

'Look at those grasshoppers, how parched!' My pink though, that came later.

By the time I was seventeen I was almost six feet tall but that was it, no more growin'. Height-wise that is. It was the time they were beginnin' to wear Afros and I had one. Four inches out which made me that much taller. Men would see me walkin' down the street and they couldn't figure what to say. Their mouths half pursed for a wolf-whistle but the sound never came out. Their eyes not quite able to imagine what my various parts might be capable of. Then, when I'd actually try to talk to them they'd hear my voice ... and I must say, it sounded like some kind of elixir some Greek god would drink to ease all kind of pain ... always did have a good voice ... and they'd shrink an inch shorter and just hang around hopin' to get petted like a little dog. I petted a few, but I was never partial to dogs.

Growin' up, my mama had always answered all those questions little girls have about men. Even my daddy. When I look back on it she was too fair on them as I see it. After she'd had me, there'd been a couple of men who she'd seen for a while, she'd told me, but they'd disappeared. She didn't say why except she'd been too busy. Once when I asked Aunt Ruby she said they'd gone away 'cause of me, 'cause they didn't wanna get mixed up with a woman who had a red-headed baby with amber eyes. When I told Ma what Aunt Ruby'd said, Ma got all quiet and her eyes became like that owl in her. Eventually she sat down close to me and ran her fingers through my hair and said, 'Sweetheart, it seems to me that most people in this world stick with whatever they think they know about, and those guys, well, they just got a little scared at what they *don't* know about. Honey, those men, they disappeared 'cause of me, not you. I guess they were just a little scared of me 'cause I wasn't what they knew about, I was different.' I remember her lookin' sad then. Then she shook her head and smiled. 'So I learned to want to see my own way through this life. Do my own thing.'

When I asked about my daddy though it was somethin' else.

She'd really get owly then, and would either get busy doin'
something or sit real still.

'You're a lot like him,' she'd say after a while. 'He was a big
man with a full head of blondish hair and a voice that filled the
air.' She told me he'd been in the Korean war. That after the war
he'd been teachin' drawin' at her college part-time in order to
support his family and continue to do his own paintings. He'd
been a married man with some kids. I didn't like what I heard. I
thought he sounded like an ace rat.

'What about his wife?' I asked her. She'd get a bit nervous
at this point, and tell me there were a lot of things that were
hard to explain but that people have all kinds of situations.
He'd been around teaching at the college for only one
semester, then gone back to Houston where he belonged. To
his wife and kids supposedly. Houston wasn't that far away
but it seemed like it then. My ma'd get all quiet again after
sayin' a couple of things about him so it'd be up to me to
keep asking. When I was younger I'd ask things like what
kind of clothes did he wear, did he have a car, did he have a
beard? Later I asked things like what'd he paint, what were
his colors like, did he draw too? I never asked, though I
thought of it all the time when I got older, if there was any
place I could see his work. The thought of actually seeing *him*
was something I got so scared of I tried hard not to think
about. But late at night I'd lie in bed, my long legs danglin'
over the edge, and I'd think, 'I bet his long legs do that too,'
and then I'd wonder where he was.

I knew his first name was Nick but I didn't know the rest of
his name. Once I asked her but she got real busy and I could tell
she didn't want to tell me. Then, after a while, I decided not to
ask because I didn't want Ma to think I might want to look him
up. Of course, lookin' back on it, she must have thought, me
becoming an artist and all, that sooner or later I'd probably run
across him. But we never talked about that. I guess we were just
too scared. Of what, beats me.

So Ma was doin' her law with the people in our little town that's gettin' to be nothin' more than a way-out suburb of sprawlin' Houston, and I manage to get accepted at the University of Houston. Two buses and an hour and a half to get there every day. I was working three afternoons a week typin' for the optometry department which I thought was dumb, except I needed the money and, besides, I figured I could learn about refraction and lenses and stuff that had to do with seeing. Not that those guys really *see*, but, in general, havin' better eyesight might help anybody. First I was takin' things like English and History and Algebra and French . . . god, I hated French . . . and P.E. and Art History which seemed, at the time, like this course about art hangin' somewhere in Europe where people stand in long lines to get in and yawn a lot. I'd go home and draw pictures of people standin' in lines or with mouths yawnin'. One thing good though, it was the first time I got to look at how different painters did light. Those professors were big on light. By then I'd got a few tubes of oil paint. There was a shed Aunt Ruby'd used out back for chickens. The chickens long-gone, I cleaned it out, strung a long extension cord out to it for a light, and started scrounging for things to paint on. First it was pieces of plywood and my drawing paper but, after I'd seen why people didn't use those too much, I managed to get some old awning canvas from Mrs Brown next door who'd decided to get venetian blinds and get rid of her awnings. Boy, those first stretchers were a hoot!

Didn't know about priming a canvas or anything like that, just figured you start painting on whatever you got. The awnings were an old faded tan so I figured I'd start with doin' browns, all shades of brown and go from there. Practice tryin' to get the light those people stood in lines in Europe to see. I'd deal with their yawnin' later.

It was January before I realized that Houston University and I were like snakes and rats . . . one ate the other . . . only I wasn't sure which one I was except I hated it. I'd found out the Houston Museum had an art school. So I took a job temping secretarial stuff and signed up for 'Basic Painting I'. I figured I already knew basic but you gotta start somewhere.

The room where it took place was in this old school, and some walls had been knocked out to make the rooms bigger, and there were some easels set up and some long tables with chairs all around. It was all kinda messy in an organized sort of way. There were about twelve students in my class including one other black person besides me and a Japanese lady. At first everybody sat around being shy or, if they knew someone, talkin' to just them. I sat there wonderin' what my eyes and hands were gonna learn next. The teacher walked in, introduced himself quickly, went over to a shelf, got down a few big books, plunked them down, opened them to certain pages he'd pre-planned and told everybody to take a look. So, we went over in our own kind of little line, not yawning. Took a look. There was one of a Picasso, then another of an O'Keeffe, and another, I think, by El Greco. We all took a look and sat back down. He turned a few more pages of the books and told us to look again. We went to look. There was a Botticelli, a Rauschenberg and a Francis Bacon. Sat down. One more time he turned the pages, said look, we lined up, looked, sat down. Then he closed the books, put them back on the shelf, put a jar full of paint brushes in the middle of the table and a rusted tin box. He said, 'Forget everything you've just seen and draw this.'

I thought of Mama. 'Not what you think you see, but what is there.'

Now I'm not sayin' I knew it all, that I did everything just right, but I knew that this teacher's and my tracks went the same way that first class. I could tell he knew it too once he saw my drawing. Didn't say anything, just peeked back over his shoulder now and then like Ma. Most of the others he made start over and over again showing them this, showing them that. But with me just the peek.

About six weeks later ... oh, we'd been drawing and painting away ... early March it must have been ... and it can get real hot

145

already in early March in Houston ... he came in with a Hawaiian shirt on with palm trees all over it and I took one look at him and hit the canvas. Did my nice palm trees and brown hula dancer, and added a moon and a star just for the hell of it, and painted black lines all around them, and then made the whole picture a shirt, a Hawaiian shirt on a light brown man with long legs and long arms and a head full of red hair the colour of rosehips tea.

He hadn't been peeking that night because one person or another had been talking to him and some other teacher had come round to discuss something with him, so he didn't see my picture till we'd almost all left. Everyone had just about cleared out, carefully moving their wet pictures to another room. I was cleaning my brushes and taking my apron off when he came over to see what I'd been up to.

His face stayed the same at first. He had a way of grinding his teeth when he was studying something. They were grinding away. He was rubbing his beard, standing there, feet apart, everything in his body quiet and still except his jaw and hands. I went over to the picture. At first I didn't say anything, just watched him lookin'.

After a couple of minutes he said, 'That supposed to be a black man or ...' he stopped. It was very clear it was a man I'd painted, not a woman. He looked at me quickly out of the corner of his eye, then back at the picture.

'I mean, is it supposed to be you if you were a man, Rae?' he asked in a confused sort of way with what I thought sounded like a little trepidation.

I sized him up fast ... 'not what you think you see, what is there' ... and I knew I had him.

'Supposed to be me if I was your son,' I paused, 'not you daughter,' I said. There was a long silence then that felt like nobody was breathing, like a cat deciding where to jump next. He leaned back on the table, put his hands in his pockets, and looked down at the floor. When he finally looked up at me his

face was real serious-looking and sorta sad, then he smiled a
little life-is-a-joke kind of smile, and shook his head back and
forth a bit.

'How is she?' he eventually said so softly I could barely hear
him. He crossed his arms over his chest.

'Oh, she's doin' good. She's a lawyer now. Real good.'

He just kept shaking his head with that funny looking smile
across his face like he was remembering some good things, and
he ground his teeth a little more. 'A lawyer, huh? She always was
smart.' Then he looked at me like he'd never seen me before. Up
and down. Assessing. Evaluating. Coming to grips I guess.
Then he turned back to the painting.

'Looks like you got more from me than my long arms and
legs,' he said, lifting his eyebrows as he stared at the picture.

'Yep,' I said. 'Looks like I got your hands. Maybe something
of your eyes too.' He stayed quiet for a while, just lookin' and
thinking. 'She always was smart, Rae.' Then he turned back to
me. 'And what about you?' he asked.

'Me?' I laughed. I turned and looked at the picture too. 'Well,
as you can see, I'm smart too, only a different smart.'

His face broke into a real smile then, and he sorta patted me
on the back and started for the door.

'C'mon,' he said. 'You wanta go get a beer or something?'

I started to take down the picture to put it in the other room.

'Leave it,' he said. 'That one needs to sit there for a while.'

So that picture eventually got moved to a studio which he found
me in a garage of a friend of his. Other things started showing up
too. Some sable brushes he'd seen me eyeing when we'd run into
each other at the art supply store . . . he'd run out of yellow ochre
and was buyin' some and saw me fondling the brushes like they
were fur coats. A book on New Guinea Aboriginal body
painting showed up too. And every now and then I'd walk into
that studio and find a canvas there . . . just when I'd been
wonderin' how I was gonna manage to afford another one. By

then I'd discovered the gallery where his work was shown. I'd hung around outside the gallery for a long time trying to get the courage to go in ... guess I was afraid I'd hate his work ... or maybe love it too much ... not sure exactly what all I was afraid of ... but I finally got the nerve up and went in. First I just walked around and looked at each painting. Then I found a chair and I ended up sitting there for about two hours just looking at his colors and his strokes. Big thick heavy ones, and just where you weren't expectin' it, some thin little line speakin' ever so softly. I just shook my head over and over, smiling like the cat that ate the mouse when the gallery lady asked if I had any questions.

Now, you might think he played some long-lost father, discoverer-of-his-daughter-the-gifted-artist role with me by the way I've set this story all up. But if you do, you got it all wrong. There was nothin' in him like that. He had his own family, his boys. And after all, I'd been alive nineteen years, and he'd never even managed to check it out. Never even seen my ma once, though I don't think he knew for sure he'd left her pregnant. I think he thought there was a possibility that she was, but she'd never contacted him either ... asking or telling anything ... so he'd never known.

So, family I was not, nor was I becoming. Fact is, I studied with him a year, then split. I'd sold a few pictures here and there, and kept doing the secretarial stuff, and lived at home with Ma, and rode the bus every day, and saved my money. And SPLIT! Wrote a postcard to him from Barcelona ... one of those pictures of the Gaudís. Also sent him a card with a Picasso rooster on it. Later, when I went to Paris I sent him another one, one of Gauguin's ladies with palm trees in the background. After I went to Europe I ended up in New York City ... near Avenue C ... five floor walk-up ... I won't go into that. But it was such a trip you wouldn't believe it ... and I got secretarial work again, and painted at night ... you know, same old story all those starving artists have at one point or another ... anyway, that went on for years. About once a year I'd see a picture of something that'd remind me of him, and I'd send it to him. Once it was one of Bacon's wrestling men, and all I wrote on the back was 'Play Serious'. But that was about it for our relationship.

But finally, around 1978, I was beginning to take off . . . for me that is . . . I was getting ready to have my first show in New York, and two of the pictures in it had already been sold before the opening. I'd moved by then to a little better place with pretty good light. I figured if the show went good, I could quit secretarial, at least go part-time, and paint all the time. Ma was coming up from home for the opening. She'd been to see me in New York before, but never to my new place, and NEVER to her only child's opening at a New York art gallery! I was Big Time! She'd been so proud to hear about it she'd arranged a whole two weeks off from her law just to be with me.

But, oh, I was gonna tell you about my pink . . . I'd found my pink by the time this show came around . . . in Italy . . . standing in a line outside the Uffizi. Well, you see, the line to go into the Uffizi was a mile long. I'd been there an hour, and still had quite a wait, and all the people were already yawnin' like you wouldn't believe . . . could just imagine how they'd be yawnin' on the inside of the place . . . and suddenly I realized that the sun was gettin' low, beginning to set. The sky was on fire! But pink fire, and by the time I was supposed to be going into the museum, I just dropped out of the line and watched the sunset instead. I went to a store the next day, and bought every colored pencil and tube of paint I could think of to work with that color. And a little canvas and some paper. And I went back to my room and painted pinks till I got my one. So now, here I was, my show full of those pinks and some of that purple-blue, and a lot of that chocolate, and some nice strokes talkin' all over the place.

Anyway, Mama showed up the afternoon of the opening, and I'd left her at my place with the understanding that she'd show up later at the gallery since I had all sorts of last-minute things to do. Well, by about nine-thirty that night I'd already shaken too many hands and nodded my head so much in replies to people I felt like somebody's dummy that got the strings crossed. Two more paintings had sold and a drawing, and my gallery owner was higher than a kite just buzzin' around all over the place. Introducing folks. Being the way gallery owners are when they gotta hustle.

I was getting tired and a little antsy about Mama showing up. I wanted to show her my stuff. I wanted to see her face and show her off to everybody. Finally I see her. She's wearing a white linen suit with a brown silk shirt on under it, and her owl eyes are smiling like her owlet has just learned to fly and is soaring above the clouds. She came up to my shoulder and just beamed into my face this smile that looked like stars in the desert at night, shining bright enough to send light a million miles away. I took her in my arms with a less-than-lady-like hug and didn't want to stop huggin' her ever. I looked down at her face. She had magic all over it and I knew she could dance on the moon. When I finally stopped hugging her and stepped back a bit to look at her, she turned a little in a peculiar sort of way as if she wanted to show me something. There, a few yards and a bunch of people away, all six-foot-five of him, was Nick. Of course, my mouth dropped open. Then I looked at Ma. Then back to Nick. Without knowing how, I moved through all those people and suddenly found myself in front of him. He was wearing a tuxedo, and I looked him up and down and realized he was wearing white tennis shoes.

'Forgot to bring my others,' he said as he saw me looking and smiling. I just looked at him and he looked back. We stood there just looking at each other for what seemed like a turn of a century. I saw myself in his eyes. He saw himself in mine. We saw each other in each other. We saw all the good things, none of the bad. He was my daddy. For once and for all. Completely this once. And I was his daughter. Completely. Forever. Mama came up beside us and hugged me again. He smiled at her and this broke the trance between us, and he shuffled a little and looked

around at all the people packin' in. His eyes got that rather itchy
look about them . . . the look he got when he wanted to move, go
into action . . . and he started grumbling.

'Hate openings,' he said, but he looked back at me to make
sure I didn't take this comment too personally. 'Never can see
the goddamn art for all the goddamn people gettin' in the way,'
he said. Then he took my arm. 'Come on,' he said looking
around him at all the people, guiding me towards another less
crowded room. Ma followed. 'I hear you make pretty good
chocolate cake,' he said, looking back at Ma. 'You gonna show
me your chocolate cake or what?'

Flipping the switch

1

'The plants need water,' was the first thing Marion said after she'd finished hugging and kissing Annie and Ginny hello. She was the kind of person who, if she saw that a plant needed water, went crazy until it got some. Ginny and Annie had flown in from L.A. five hours earlier but hadn't got round to watering the drooping aspidistra and withering croton in the front bay window. It would have been over a week since the plants had been watered because their mother had gone into the hospital on a Wednesday night and now it was another Wednesday night.

Ginny's baby toddled into the room and Marion picked her up. She'd seen her only a few months before but baby Rachel hadn't been walking then. Life happens fast, Marion thought as she looked at her. One day you're crawling around, the next day you're walking. Then she thought of her mother. One day she was walking to the grocery store, trying to remember the names of those people who moved in on the corner, the next day she found herself in a hospital. A few days later the doctors said they wanted to put her in an old age home – and she died. Massive heart attack on the spot.

That's how Carrie had done it. Just flipped the switch to off.

'Oh, Mom, you're here thirty seconds and the first thing you notice is that the plants need water,' Annie said, smiling. Marion put down the baby and hugged Annie again. If there were any good points to any of this, Marion thought, at least she got to be with Annie for a while.

'Are you hungry?' Ginny asked.

'God, I'm starved!' Marion followed Ginny into the kitchen and Annie picked up the baby and came behind.

'I thought we might all need a good meal so I went out and bought some food,' Ginny said, opening the refrigerator door to show Marion. It brimmed with packages and containers of food, bowls covered in waxed paper held with rubber bands, baking pans wrapped in aluminium foil. 'Mine's the stuff that doesn't have six inches of mold growing on it,' she heaved a sigh and pointed. Marion poked her head around the door.

'Oh, god, can you believe it? Look, there's that Christmas pudding from Marks and Spencer's I sent her and Daddy three years ago.' She felt a twinge of sadness at the thought of her mother and father looking at the directions on the package of the English Christmas pudding she'd sent them, then deciding maybe they'd boil it up later, then never finding the enthusiasm to get around to doing it. She should have known better than to send it to them in the first place. After all, they never had been very interested in trying new things.

She looked around the kitchen. 'Got a trash bag started?' Ginny pointed to a black plastic bag and Marion dragged it over to the refrigerator and dropped the Christmas pudding into it. She started with the side doors and began throwing out jars of relish, jam, packets of mayonnaise left over from a café years ago ... probably whenever some relative had last taken Carrie out for lunch ... opened packages of bologna, green at the edges.

'Mom, you can do that later,' Annie said, putting Rachel down.

'Have you heard from Aunt Ellie?' Marion ignored Annie.

'Yeah, she called. You're supposed to phone her and Aunt Lil after a while. They've already arranged everything.'

Marion went over to the sink to get a sponge to start cleaning out the gunge at the bottom of the vegetable tray.

'Mom, why don't you just *sit down* for a few minutes!' Annie took the sponge from her mother's hand, threw it in the sink and led her back into the den. They sat down on the sofa. Annie's golden hair gleamed in squeaky cleanness. Marion reached over to touch it, this wonderful gold her daughter possessed. Annie was her baby, her youngest one, grown up and gone off to college. But she was still Marion's little girl, and she closed her eyes as Marion caressed her, then she reached out and took her hand. They squeezed tightly, the love between them as it had always been, a strong current on the same frequency.

'Your hands,' Annie said. 'They're just like Grandmommie's.' Annie held Marion's hand in both of hers and examined its surface veins, its long, skinny fingers, the wrinkles of skin jutting up and between the bones. Little old lady hands. 'I'm getting them too,' Annie said as she turned one of her hands palm down and held it next to Marion's for comparison.

2

'That's a nice suit,' Marion said as Ginny came out of the back room. The night before, Marion had been really surprised when Ginny said she wanted to sleep in the back room with Rachel, in their parents' old room. It had made complete sense, of course, because it was the largest bedroom and Ginny could spread out her and the baby's things. But Marion couldn't imagine sleeping in that room herself. It was so *full* of Carrie still. And even though Annie had helped Ginny make up the bed with fresh sheets, even with Ginny's and Rachel's suitcases and clothes and toys covering every surface, the room was still full of her.

'It's a good thing it has a jacket,' Ginny said, breaking Marion out of her reflections, fiddling with the zipper at the back of her skirt. 'I haven't lost all my weight from when I was pregnant.'

Ginny noticed Marion's navy blue and white print dress. 'I like your dress. It's very English.'

Marion looked down at what she was wearing. 'It is, isn't it? I bought it second-hand when I had to go to a wedding last year. I remember trying to decide between it and another one which had a lot of bright colors and thinking at the time that I could ... wear this for a funeral if I ever had to.'

Ginny sat down in the rocker and took Rachel into her lap. She began putting shoes and socks on Rachel's tiny feet.

'I know.' She didn't look at Marion but concentrated on Rachel's shoes. 'I knew it was going to happen too.'

Annie came into the room, dressed and ready to go, which roused Marion into hurrying into the bathroom to finish getting ready.

The doorbell rang just as she applied her lipstick. The morning before ... well, it seemed like the morning before, although the time difference between London and Texas made it more like two days before ... as Marion had scurried about London buying tickets and drawing out money from the bank, she'd stopped by Boots to get some antihistamines and passed the cosmetics bar. Although she wore make-up, Marion usually avoided wearing lipstick. It was too bright, placed too much emphasis on the lips. Strangely enough, it was about the only cosmetic her mother always used. She could remember her mother hounding her about it for years. 'Don't you want a little color on your face?' she would say. 'You look so pale.'

'I never wear lipstick, Mother, you know that. I haven't worn lipstick since the sixties.'

'The sixties!' Carrie would spit out and an awful sneer would cover her face like a dog about ready to attack its natural enemy.

So, Marion had bought a lipstick. She couldn't help but wonder what other things she would begin to do differently now. What things, for that matter, she would never *have* to do again. For one thing, she'd never have to fight with Carrie again. She'd never have to get upset when Carrie used the word 'nigger', she'd never have to stand up for hispanics, or homosexuals, or anti-nuclear protesters, or people who drank alcohol, or women who showed their cleavages on TV.

Annie answered the door and let in Aunt Lil and Uncle Sid. Ginny and Marion greeted them with hugs. Baby Rachel captured their attention and the initial awkwardness of the occasion was blunted by their focus upon her. Marion thought, thank god, thank god for that. The baby would distract, keep the focus away from them. Marion listened as Ginny and Aunt Lil talked about the baby and Uncle Sid asked his usual questions of Annie. How was college? How was Hollywood? Seen any movie stars lately? Marion quickly retreated to the bathroom with the excuse that she had to finish getting ready. She ran the brush through her hair one last time and stuffed a few tissues into her bag. But, as she was about ready to go back out, something stopped her and she looked in the mirror. She was alarmed at first. She hadn't seen that person in the mirror for quite some time. She smiled at her, this old friend, the one who had cried with her in this same bathroom so many times before on previous visits back home. She noticed once again that her friend in the mirror had eyes like Carrie's, eyes like Carrie's mother's – Alexandra, Marion's daughter back home in London had them too. They got passed down like family jewels. Over the years those eyes in the mirror had laughed at how seriously Marion took everything her mother said. But they had also taken seriously any laughter she managed to find along the way. Here we go, those eyes said to Marion now. To your mother's funeral. Here we go.

Annie, Ginny, Rachel and Marion piled into the back of Aunt Lil and Uncle Sid's yellow Lincoln Continental. Carrie had thought their car was the most beautiful car in the whole world and she never missed an opportunity to comment on it even though it was over fifteen years old by now.

As they turned into the parking lot of the funeral home Aunt Lil started spotting those who had already arrived by recogniz-

ing their cars. There were at least five cousins and four aunts and
uncles she knew were there by the presence of their parked cars.
They drove into the covered area and pulled up behind the
hearse. Several men, wearing black suits and practiced expressions of sympathy, hovered nearby. An acid taste filled Marion's
mouth and her jaws set firmly. Here were the professional death
men. She ground her teeth to keep the words inside. Funeral
biz. Another closing, another show.

The men opened the doors to the Lincoln and they got out of
the car. Some words were exchanged between one of the men
and Uncle Sid and he gestured towards Marion. The man came
over and introduced himself as the director of the funeral home.
He explained he understood that she was the oldest daughter,
and the executor, and he wanted to offer his condolences. If he
could be of any help in any way . . .

Executor was the operative word here, Marion almost said out
loud to him. Executor of the will. The one who pays for things
like the funeral. She found herself wanting to stare at the man
and look away at the same time. His eyes were gray coins and she
was sure if she were ever in the appalling position of actually
having to smell his breath it would most likely resemble rotting
chrysanthemums.

They were ushered into the side of the chapel allotted for
family. Ginny, Annie and Marion nodded and attempted smiles
as they recognized each cousin, each uncle and aunt. They sat on
the front row and looked out at the rest of the mourners.

Marion forced herself to look at all those who'd come, to
assess the wrinkled packages of faces of the women in her
mother's Sunday school class, marvel at the ancient, balding
second cousins, the brown, leathery skins of her father's old golf
buddies. Then there were the flowers to notice, the sprays of
lilies, wreaths of roses, pots of coleus. She focused upon the non-
descript architecture of the building, the wood panelling, the
moss green material covering the seats of the pews. She
searched the room for an escape; she was a moth knowing where

the light was, but resisting it frantically. She knew, of course, exactly where she would have to look eventually, where Carrie would be. She would be in an open casket on a platform in front of everyone. Finally, when she could stand it no longer, she looked. Finally there Carrie was. But there she *wasn't* really, not really. Something was there alright, dressed in a suit Marion had never seen before.

She was too far away to see very well, but Marion could tell they'd tried to fix Carrie's hair to look right. But how could they? It hadn't looked right for at least ten years. Carrie had refused to have it done in a beauty parlor, refused to have anybody touch it. She'd colored it herself using the same auburn tint she'd used for over thirty years. 'Loving Care' was the product's name. Marion remembered this now and couldn't help smiling. As Carrie had aged her eyesight had worsened and she'd miss great patches at the back and crown of her head. Originally, when she'd started dyeing her hair in her forties, she'd said she was doing it for Marion's father and, half-jokingly, he'd agreed. 'Don't want no gray-haired old lady for *my* wife,' he'd say. But back then there'd only been a few gray hairs and, as the years went by and it all turned gray and thinned, the tint had done funny things to it. Carrie had ended up with hair that looked like Lucille Ball starring in 'Whatever Happened to Baby Jane'.

It didn't look like that now though. They'd done something to it.

The taped music in the background, a selection of various hymns played on an organ, got softer as the minister from the First Baptist Church entered from a side door. He took his place next to the coffin as another church man took his place next to him. At this point the uncles and cousins and other relatives and friends grew silent. The music faded. The minister asked everyone to bow their heads in prayer.

Marion leaned over and whispered to Ginny. 'Ya da ya da ya da.'

Ginny shot a quick glance at her and smiled.

'You got it,' Ginny whispered back.

'Wanna place any bets on the choice of hymns?'

'"Old Rugged Cross",' Ginny said, not missing a beat.

'Right. Then, "In the Garden".' Ginny nodded. 'And the last one?' They looked at each other and simultaneously mouthed 'Amazing Grace' and fought for just a second to keep from giggling. Annie, who was sitting on the other side of Marion, elbowed her. When Marion looked over at her, Annie gave her a fake glare. Marion knew Annie understood this stuff between the two sisters but Marion also knew Annie was right. It would have to keep until later, whatever this urge towards black comedy was about.

3

The first thing they all did when they got back to the house was kick off their shoes. Everyone and his brother would be coming round now. The doorbell began to ring almost as soon as they'd stepped in the door, with neighbors bringing casseroles, baked ham, lemon sponge cake, jello fruit salads, dutch apple pies. Aunt Lil started a list of names and a description of each item brought so that thank you notes could be sent later. Marion hoped no one brought a lemon pie. No one could make a lemon meringue pie like her mother used to. The phone started ringing. Soon the house would be packed full of people, something that hadn't happened since their father's death two and a half years before.

Marion let Annie answer the phone and Aunt Dee Dee the door and she headed for the bathroom. She locked the door behind her, leaned against the vanity and stared into the mirror again. They weren't there, she said to her friend in the mirror. The family jewels, her mother's eyes, had been closed.

After the ceremony, everyone had filed by the open casket as Ginny, Annie and Marion waited. In England they didn't have open caskets. Marion thought that this rather primitive practice must be some strange American take on things.

Then, after the others had left, Ginny, the baby, Annie and Marion were led towards the casket. Yes, this was what came next, Marion told herself. This was what happened. You got a phone call in the middle of the night, you lay on your bed and cried as long as you could, then you packed your bags, flew home, got up the next morning, got dressed, were driven to a chapel, sat through the service, and, at last, were led to the casket to see your mother for the last time. She watched as Ginny touched the body's hand, then its cheek. Ginny's lips moved slightly, then baby Rachel started to wiggle, demanding her attention, so Ginny moved along, towards the door.

It was just her now, though Annie stood nearby, crying, waiting to comfort. She stepped closer to the casket and it occurred to her suddenly that she might actually laugh. If the body looked absurdly made-up, entirely un-lifelike, like a wax figure in Madame Tussaud's, she might laugh.

The face resembled Carrie's but it was too round, puffy. The jaw was too firm as though, in death, her teeth had grown to fill out the back of her mouth. The lines on her face were still there but softer. Somebody who didn't know her as well might have concluded the softness meant a peacefulness. That Carrie was resting in peace. But Marion knew better. Carrie was just *gone* was what Carrie was. Nobody there. No answer. Disconnected. Out.

Knowing her mother, peace would have been the last thing on her mind. She would have wanted to get on with finding her departed husband on 'the other side'. Find her own mother, her own father, all those old great-uncles and aunts and cousins who died years ago. Have that monumental family-reunion-in-the-sky, eating yellow-meat watermelon out on a lawn in heaven – a lawn next to the streets paved in gold, of course – and there would be a light breeze, no mosquitoes and nothing but forever to talk about. Marion wondered, if this heaven of Carrie's really did exist, how long would it take before Carrie started worrying about how she was going to get her and Ginny and Annie and all the rest up to heaven with her. It was for sure she worried about that often enough before she died.

'I'm just worried to death,' Carrie screamed in tears one night during Marion's last visit, 'that we won't be together in heaven.'

Marion was caught off guard as usual, but kept herself from reacting this time. She couldn't remember exactly when she'd learned to control her reactions. It had been a relatively recent development though because, over the last few years, as her mother became more and more disoriented and *obviously* crazy – as opposed to her normal crazy – it became a little easier to distance herself, to drive a wedge between what she felt and what her mother was screaming at her.

'Now, Mama. I think you have more important things to worry about than that. It'll be all right.'

'There's nothin' more important than that.'

'Well, you don't have to worry, I'll be there,' Marion lied. If there was one thing she *didn't* want, it was to end up in a heaven that even remotely resembled the one her mother dreamt of. That would be *hell* for Marion. But then, of course, Carrie believed Marion was going to go to hell anyway.

Marion sometimes thought that heaven might be whatever one wanted it to be. But if that was the case, Carrie would never have it exactly like she wanted it because Marion would never want to be in her mother's heaven. Carrie's idea of heaven was like a Victorian greeting card. Lambs jumping around in perfect daisy-covered fields, and the great Jesus-shepherd touching all their heads and smiling down upon them daily, giving them a sense of overwhelming euphoria.

Marion could visualize euphoria well enough. Sometimes when she tried to get to sleep at night she imagined things that would make her feel really good. What, in other words, her heaven would be like. First of all, they'd pass a pipe of very good opium, then maybe a line or two. Then, this wonderful guy who'd look a lot like Al Pacino and who would understand everything she felt on the deepest of levels and sympathize totally, would come over and make love to her. Annie and Alexandra would be somewhere nearby having a party with their friends. The Beatles, the Stones, Clapton, Elton John, Billy Joel, Paul Simon and others would be playing in the background.

There would be no black people in Carrie's heaven. They'd have their own section. Or Mexicans. In fact, there'd only be white Americans with possibly a few Brits mixed in. The men would be the bosses of course, and they'd play dominoes at night after the women went to bed.

Whereas, in Marion's heaven, there would be no bosses, male or otherwise, or Southern Baptists, or orthodox, fundamentalist anythings. Jesus would play a guitar alongside Buddha and everyone would have a tan.

4

Annie knocked on the bathroom door. 'Mom, Big Marion's here.' Marion clicked herself back into gear with the moment and winked goodbye to the mirror.

Big Marion was Marion's second cousin for whom she'd been named. As a little girl, Big Marion had been Carrie's favourite cousin. Big Marion was from the side of Carrie's family that had money, and she was always dressed in the prettiest clothes, had piano lessons, went to university – all the things Carrie thought meant 'class'. But Marion had never known her cousin because Marion's parents had moved away from the little town before Marion had been born. It was only after her parents returned to live in this town, many years after Marion had left home, that

Marion was ever around Big Marion at all. Over the years, on trips back to visit her parents, Big Marion had come round to visit and Marion had begun to pick up on various clues that her cousin was actually someone she might feel proud to be named after.

They smiled and threw their arms around each other.

'How you doin', kid,' Big Marion said softly.

'Oh, you know.'

'Yeah, I know.' Marion followed as Big Marion walked into the den where others mingled, sampling the food laid out on the tables. She greeted each familiar face with her usual charming, self-confident smile and went about shaking hands with the men, kissing the women on their cheeks, breaking the ice of the somewhat sombre occasion. After a few minutes, a cup of coffee in one hand and a piece of cake in the other, she sidled back over to Marion. The doorbell was ringing constantly at this point and more people were coming in.

'We're not gonna be able to talk with all this, are we?' she whispered as she looked around. 'God, I'd like a beer right now.' She winked at Marion and Marion laughed. 'Look, when do Annie and Ginny and the baby leave?'

'Saturday I think.'

'And how long will you be here?'

'Till I can take care of everything that has to be done. A few weeks.'

'OK, so after they leave, plan to stay over with me a couple of nights.'

'I'd love that.' Marion had the feeling that when she finally got to spend time with Big Marion, it would be the closest she'd ever come to finding anything around here that even remotely resembled a world she could relate to on her own terms.

She gave Big Marion a hug, took a deep breath and set about greeting the new arrivals. She repeated, over and over again, the same things. Yes, she'd arrived from London the night before. Yes, she was sorry Alexandra couldn't make it over from

England but she was in the middle of her term at University and it was so expensive to fly and ... Yes, it was cold in England. Yes, she sometimes missed America. No, her husband couldn't take time off from work to come. Well, thanks, of course everyone would miss her. Yes, it really was for the best. Yes, Carrie was at peace now. She was better off. She was with her husband and father and mother now. She would suffer no more. Yes, she had been so pitiful in the end. Yes, she felt bad that she hadn't been able to ... but ... she was sorry ... she felt terribly guilty ... she tried to ... there was food over there on the table.

5

'Want a beer?' Big Marion asked as she got herself one out of the fridge and snapped the pop-top.

'Sure.' Marion could barely believe she was actually going to be able to sit down and have an alcoholic drink with a relative. In all her adult years she'd never once been around anyone in the family who'd even offered her one. And since her mother, whenever they were in the presence of other relations, had always hovered around her like some great old hen watching her chick's every move, she supposed she would have had to fight to accept one even if it had been offered. She remembered how her father used to sneak out to the garage to take a nip of the cheap wine he hid under the driver's seat of the car. How he'd always come home from the golf course with beer on his breath. But what she remembered most was how her mother reacted to his drinking. She'd become indignant, heaving sigh after sigh. She'd start rustling dishes in the sink in the kitchen and slamming cabinet doors. She wouldn't speak a word to him and only after dinner, when he'd settled down in front of the TV for a nap, would she soften and go about her business cleaning up the kitchen. Of course, there were those other times when they'd actually scream and shout at each other. Times when he'd actually hit her, he'd be so angry. But in spite of this, in spite of how much Carrie hated his drinking and went on and on at him about it, she never admitted that anyone else in the family ever touched a drop.

So now Marion was sitting in Big Marion's house, drinking a beer and smoking cigarettes. She could look out at the lake, relax and then maybe, if she was lucky, she'd get to hear some of the stories she'd been waiting for. Some of Big Marion's.

Carrie's stories – those great myths of the ancestors, with southern belles from Georgia marrying confederate captains and pioneering and settling Texas – had been drilled into Ginny's and Marion's heads from earliest memory. The log cabin where her great-grandmother bore six sons and six daughters, their conquering of the nearby Comanches. Marion used to love all these stories until she moved away from home. Then, over the years, she'd begun to wonder.

'They were all drunks, of course,' Big Marion started talking in her gravelly soft voice, exhaling a drag off her cigarette. 'Drunks and most of them as mean as the devil. Your daddy, Uncle Sid, also your Uncle Chuck – god, he's the worst – my daddy, even my *husband*, for god's sake, all of them as pickled as cucumbers. Oh, I don't mean they all stay or stayed drunk all the time, but they drink a lot. Your Uncle Sid, for instance. I bet he starts hittin' it around three every day and stays that way. God knows when your Uncle Chuck starts. Probably at breakfast.'

'So, your husband too?' Marion asked shyly, surprised. She had never known Big Marion's husband.

'I'm afraid Brad, bless his dear jaded little heart, could drink with the best of them. Even mother, my own mother, drank like a fish. She chose vodka, of course, 'cause you couldn't smell it on her breath. I mean, how else could they manage in a place like this, you know?' Big Marion chuckled a chesty, sardonic laugh. 'After all, you had your work cut out for you, didn't you! You had to keep those niggers in their place, make sure that Mexican man mowed your lawn right and didn't overcharge you, make sure no white trash family with snot-nosed kids moved in on the next street, keep those anti-war hippie communist agitators out of town and, most importantly of all, hold your head up high as a fine, upstanding Christian American *rock* every Sunday at church. It was hard work but, damn it, somebody had to do it!' Big Marion looked out at the lake which lay at the bottom of the yard that stretched out beneath the picture window of her living room.

'But was Brad like that too?' Marion remembered hearing some kind of gossip about Brad from somebody.

'Boy, you really have led a sheltered life,' Big Marion laughed again.

'Well, Mama never talked about him,' Marion explained. 'She just always talked about how pretty you looked or how your sister was doing. Of course, I knew *something* was going on when Mama let it slip one time that your father wasn't speaking to your son. I mean, that time I saw him in the sixties and he had long hair, and everybody said he was a draft dodger and all.' Marion grinned rather sheepishly. 'I have to admit, when I saw him during that time, I thought I might have *somebody* in the family I could relate to.'

Big Marion smiled at that but her smile faded fast. 'Can you believe that my father wouldn't speak to David for five whole years during that time! Five years! You wouldn't have known I guess, but, you see, David was a conscientious objector during the Vietnam War and he was given a job in the worst ghetto in New York City for three years. But in spite of this, my good ol' Patriot, World War I Veteran of a daddy wouldn't speak to him. Brad defended him completely of course so, as a result, my daddy wouldn't speak to him either. But it wasn't the first time my daddy didn't speak to Brad. Or to me for that matter. He tried to disinherit me at least three times in the early sixties when Brad and I started getting involved with the Civil Rights stuff up in Killeen. If it hadn't been for the fact he was afraid for my life, he probably would have ended up actually going through with it.'

'What do you mean, afraid for your life?'

'Well, you see, Brad and I and several of our friends were helping the blacks get legal counseling. We were telling them their rights and getting them to vote, finding them places to stay when they got into trouble, bailing them out of jail, all that. Eventually we started getting threats. Then one night this friend of ours came over in the middle of the night and said we had to get out of there. A group of rednecks who hated our guts had paid the sheriff to look the other way and they'd put out the word that if we weren't out by the next morning, they were coming to get us. So we sent the kids to stay with my parents, and Brad and I filled our car with as many things as we could cram into it and we came here. At that time, this was all just a piece of land by the lake that Daddy had bought years before as an investment. So we camped out here. As it turned out, they burned down our house in Killeen, so we just stayed here. Eventually we built this house and Brad continued to commute back and forth to Killeen. He never gave up.'

'I never knew any of that.' Marion slumped in her chair, unable to process all this information. Somehow she felt it all meant something about who she was. Suddenly she was more than just the daughter of a remnant of a faded aristocracy, more than the daughter, cousin, niece, of a bunch of drunks. She was somebody who'd been named for somebody who stood for all she really believed in.

As Big Marion continued, Marion let her mind spread out and claim little bits and pieces of the world she'd come from but had never really known. One part of her brain took in the new information as other parts tried to figure out what it all meant, what it added up to. Finally, she drew back into focus upon her mother. What did all this that Big Marion was talking about have to do with her? Where had she fit into it all?

There was a pause now and neither of them spoke as they looked out on the lake, watched the occasional bird fly by.

'You know, thinking about it all now,' Marion finally spoke, 'my mother must have been even more deluded than I thought. I mean, I always knew she was pretty screwed-up, that she never lived in the "real world", so to speak. But, to listen to her, you were absolutely perfect. You could do no wrong. It's like she created this fantasy to believe in, to try to make *us* believe in. And she really *did* believe all that stuff she made up. I mean why? How could she?'

Big Marion shook her head. It was a movement of both agreement and understanding. 'Well, honey, I don't know. I really don't. I've thought about it so often.' Then she turned and smiled at Marion. 'But I always loved your mother. I never could understand what was *wrong* with her maybe but she was always so sweet – crazy as a loon maybe – but so sweet!' She went over to the fridge and got another beer.

'Want another one?' Marion shook her head no. Her mood had changed and she now had no desire to dull her thinking processes. Big Marion flipped the tab off the top of the beer and came back and sat down again.

'You know, I always thought that maybe what was wrong with your mother had something to do with when she got tuberculosis all those years ago, and her mother being sick with it herself. And Carrie having to be like a little mother to her three younger brothers. I think that's why my daddy loved her so much, 'cause he felt so sorry for her and because she was his sister's only daughter.'

Marion nodded. 'Yeah, all that's a part of it. She once told me that from the time she was twelve years old she woke up every morning wondering if her mother was still alive. Did she ever tell you the story about when she found out about her own tuberculosis?'

'No, I never did hear about that. She never brought it up and I guess I was too embarrassed to ask.'

'Well, she was nineteen and at the swimming pool with a bunch of her friends, and she'd been swimming and when she got out of the pool she started to cough up blood. So, she ended up in the sanitarium with her mother for a year. Then, after she got well and came back, she said all her old friends just disappeared. She blamed it on the TB. She said they were scared they'd get it.' Recalling this to Big Marion made Marion flash on another more recent memory. 'You know, the last time I was here I was trying to get her to talk about the old days and I brought up the swimming pool story to her and, can you believe it, she denied the whole thing! She acted like I'd just made it up. She got so upset that she had to go take a nap.' Big Marion chuckled at this. 'But getting back to the friends part of all this, my mother never *did* have any friends.'

'I know,' Big Marion answered, shaking her head. 'Never let anyone do anything for her or get close enough to her to talk about anything deeper than the weather.' She looked at Marion over the beer can as she took another swig. Something in her posture seemed to change then. 'But what I can't figure out is how you and Ginny turned out so good. I mean how you turned out so *normal*! I'll never, for the life of me, know how that happens.'

'Normal?' Marion laughed at the thought of that word being applied to her life.

'Well, you know what I mean. You live in the real world. You have two beautiful daughters who're great, from what I can tell, and you work, you have a nice husband, you live in *London*! I mean, you're real and not as neurotic as hell!'

'Oh, I don't know about that last part.' Marion arched her left eyebrow in a maybe-if-you-knew-me-better kind of expression and looked away. 'Sometimes I think I'm just like her, like I picked up all her worst traits.'

Big Marion sighed and nodded as if she understood. 'I think we all feel like that sometimes, like we're gonna end up being just like our mothers. But that's silly. We have a whole set of different circumstances and experiences than they did. You can't just focus upon all the bad things. You have to look at all the other stuff too.'

6

Marion spent the next couple of weeks dealing with the lawyer, putting the house on the market, paying bills. She arranged to have some of the furniture and other items sent out to Ginny and Annie in Los Angeles. Then, with Big Marion's and Aunt Lil's help, she started organizing and labelling all the rest of Carrie's possessions which she decided she would have to get rid of in an estate sale. This took days of tedious labor during which she would not allow herself to stop. It wasn't just that she had very little time off from work, she was aware that stopping could be emotionally fatal. There were closets of clothes, of papers, newspaper cuttings, letters – Carrie had saved every Mother's Day card, every Christmas card, every Valentine she'd ever received in her whole life and each one brought back a memory that Marion quickly acknowledged but prohibited herself from succumbing to emotionally. In all, she hauled thirty trash bags full of papers and letters and other things out for the garbage men to pick up. She made Big Marion and Aunt Lil take whatever they wanted from all her mother's things. She gave the six Bibles she'd found throughout the house to the Baptist church. She paid the damned funeral home. She arranged to have the phone cut off when the time came. She put an ad in the newspaper about the estate sale. Finally, the day of the estate sale came and Aunt Lil and Big Marion arrived at seven-thirty in the morning. There was already a throng of people waiting outside the garage door. She'd put up signs the night before, telling people not to ring the door bell, that the sale would start at eight o'clock.

The plan was that one of them would be in the house at all times and one in the garage. The other would go back and forth. Earlier in the week Aunt Lil and Aunt Ellie and various other relatives had warned her about the people who'd be showing up, about how she would have to watch everything like a hawk, especially when the Mexicans showed up. Marion bit her lip and choked back the words she wanted to reply. She knew it was useless to say anything, that these women who were in their late sixties had spent their whole lives thinking the way they did and they would continue to do so and there was nothing she could do to change that. Just like she could never change her mother. But she also noticed how neither of her aunts ever made such statements when Big Marion was around.

The people rushed in and started buying. They bought the horrible pottery she'd made when she took that ceramics course in the seventies and gave pieces to her mother for Christmas. They bought old bottles and shoe racks and wooden tables and bookcases. They bought boxes of lawn fertilizer and pillow cases and tools and Christmas decorations. They bought Easter baskets and old cutlery and cups without saucers. They bought the instant coffee maker without a cord and an ironing board without its cover. A cousin showed up and bought the washer and dryer. A man and his wife who were moving to town from Dallas had heard about the sale when they'd opened an account at the bank. They ended up buying her parents' king-sized bed, a chest of drawers, a coffee table and a few plants.

It was mid-afternoon when Mr Gonzales showed up. Mr Gonzales was the Mexican-American man who had always mowed Carrie's lawn. Carrie had been very fond of him in her last months of life – even though he was a 'Mexican' – because he always asked how she was feeling and tried to help her by doing little extra things around the house. In fact, he had been the one who had discovered Carrie when she'd had her last two heart attacks. It was he who had found her unconscious on the bathroom floor the last time.

Marion said hello to him warmly, then noticed the look in his eye. He was an old man, in his early seventies she guessed, and Marion couldn't help but feel he didn't like her. She watched as he looked through the things that were laid out on tables, picked up a tool or two and put them back down. His grandson, a large man in his twenties, followed behind him and they spoke to each other in Spanish every now and then. Eventually the old man came over to her.

'Your mother was a nice lady,' he said and looked away at all the things in the garage. She could see he'd like to say more but could not find the words.

'She liked you very much, Mr Gonzales,' she said. He looked back at her and didn't reply but the expression on his face was one of admonishment, of cold critical judgement. Marion thought she knew what he would have said if he'd been able to. 'Your mother would not like you doing this,' he would say. 'Selling all her things, even her clothes. And where were you when your mother needed you? Your mother was sick and old and alone and you weren't there.' The words she saw in his face circled and blended with all the other words in her mind, the memories of past arguments, of her mother's tortured, depressive outlook on life. They fitted themselves among other thoughts, other memories of how her parents had taken the news that she was marrying an Englishman and going off to live in England, of her father's death a few years later, of her mother learning to write checks for the first time at age seventy-five. Of the phone calls made from England once a month when she'd ask Carrie how she was feeling and Carrie would answer, 'Not worth shootin'.'

At that point Big Marion poked her head out of the kitchen and into the garage.

'Mrs Salter wants to know how much you want for these blankets,' she said, not having any way of knowing how much Marion needed to be rescued. She went into the house to deal with the woman who was interested in the blankets. She sold her the blankets and another lady, a box of buttons. A young couple bought the single bed and a lamp. A few minutes later she came back into the den to find Mr Gonzales and his grandson looking at the sewing machine. They had lifted it up out of the case that it folded down into, which doubled as a table. They were inspecting the motor.

'How much you want for this?' Mr Gonzales asked in a monotone voice. She tried to think but all she could come up with was feelings. She walked over to Mr Gonzales and stood close to him.

'I think my mother would want you to have this sewing machine, Mr Gonzales.' He looked at her, then at his grandson and said something in Spanish. He backed away from her slightly.

'It's for my wife,' he said, not acknowledging her offer. 'Will you take twenty dollars?' He reached into his pocket for his wallet. Her first impulse was to repeat her offer but she stopped herself. Mr Gonzales was not going to be bought. Mr Gonzales wanted to pay and wanted her to pay too.

7

Marion's cousin, Bill, had bought the television set, the refrigerator and the mattress and arranged to pick them up the day she left. She had a couple more days of running around to do – seeing the lawyer again, going to the bank, signing forms for the real estate people – before she'd be on her way back to England. Most of the next day she planned to clean the empty house.

But tonight she was going to eat the tamales Aunt Ellie had brought over, take a long, hot bath, then settle down on that mattress and watch television and not move her bones again for as long as she could possibly stand it.

She was just about to draw the bath when Annie called from L.A. Then Ginny called. She found herself describing in great detail all the events of the recent days gone by, allowing herself to shed a few tears when Annie asked if it had hit her yet, her mother's death. But they were only a few tears; she couldn't let it all out now. There was no time. It would just have to come later, she told Annie, when she got back to England, when everything was done, finished. Annie seemed to understand, but there was a cautiousness in her voice that Marion knew was Annie worrying.

She hung up and headed for the bathroom and the phone rang again. This time it was Jean, another cousin. Jean was five years older than Marion, the two had never been close, but she had always been another relative Marion had wondered about.

Jean started out asking about the sale and went on from there asking about everything else in Marion's life. Marion did the same. They had talked for almost an hour when the subject of alcoholism came up. Jean was Uncle Chuck's daughter, the one Big Marion had said probably got up in the morning and started hitting the booze. Marion listened in amazement as Jean described her years of psychotherapy, the years of meetings with her Adult Child of an Alcoholic group, her divorce from her alcoholic husband, her sadness over her son's drinking and joy over his eventual rehabilitation.

As she sat there, her ear growing numb from constant contact with the receiver of the phone, her body aching from the day's, the week's work, she felt something inside her ease a notch, as though a scab from a wound had just fallen off. She felt lighter, softer. What wound was this? Where on her body was it? Were there others?

When she eventually hung up, pledging to keep in touch, it was ten o'clock. She drew the curtains across the sliding doors to the den, and went into the bathroom to turn on the water. She took off her clothes and eased herself into the bath. She did not have to lock the bathroom door or draw the shower curtain around the tub anymore for fear that her mother would pop into the bathroom unexpectedly and see her body. She lay in the tub and closed her eyes and remembered her last visit. One hot afternoon they'd been sitting in the den watching television when Carrie suddenly stood up and came over to her. She was smiling a crazy, otherworldly smile, as if whatever she was thinking had nothing to do with what she was trying to show Marion as she began to hike up her skirt.

'I thought you'd like to feel my lump,' she said and, before Marion could pull back, Carrie reached over and grabbed her hand and put it on her groin. She rubbed Marion's hand across the skin just at the right of her pubic area where a large bump had appeared recently. As soon as Marion could release her hand, she drew it back in a reflex action. Carrie picked up on her repulsion at having touched her.

'Not that you care or anything,' she sneered, her face suddenly becoming mean and wild-looking.

'Well, of course I care,' Marion snapped back, but Carrie knew Marion had been repulsed and it was too late for her to try to act otherwise. 'Have you been to the doctor about it?'

'Doctor!' Carrie spat. 'Nah, I haven't "been to the doctor about it,"' she imitated Marion's voice, but made it a whining, sissy little-girl's voice. 'And I'm not going to either. You can't make me. *They* don't care. Nobody cares. Nobody except your dear departed father ever gave a good d in hell about me.' Carrie always used the letter 'd' as a substitute for the word damn.

'Oh, Mother, you know that's not true. I care for you. Ginny cares, Annie and Alexandra care. A lot of others around here care too.'

With that Carrie went off on a tirade about how everyone hated her, how no one had ever cared, how she couldn't stand the old lady on the soap opera they'd been watching, how everybody was trying to get her to go to those senior citizen lunches with all those old, common people, how she didn't want anything to eat for supper, how the world was going to hell, how she was glad she wouldn't be around to see it when it happened, and how she only hoped, only prayed with every ounce of her body that Marion would end up in heaven with her one day. Finally she took herself off into the bedroom for a nap.

She hadn't always been like that, Marion tried to remind herself. But the more she tried to remember her mother in better days, the harder it became. All she could think of were all the bad things, none of the good.

As she got out of the tub and started to dry off, the phone rang again. She ran into the den to answer it, but by the time she got there, the caller had hung up. She stood there in the den and looked around. She had left the towel in the bathroom and was absolutely naked. The room was empty except for the television, the mattress on the floor and her suitcases. The whole house was empty except for those things and the refrigerator in the kitchen. She took a few timid steps towards the kitchen, looking first to make sure all the curtains were drawn and the doors to the other rooms closed. She turned on the television. The theme tune to MASH was playing. She turned the sound up loud and, before she knew what she was doing, she started dancing.

'Are you watching?' she said out loud. For a moment she flashed on the thought that she might be going crazy, talking out loud to herself, but she continued anyway. 'You can't really look down from up there, can you?' she laughed as she started to cry. 'Well, if you can, then you can see that I'm not wearing anything. See? Nothing at all.' She danced around the room a little more. 'Marion, you should be ashamed of yourself,' she mocked her mother's voice. Then she laughed again and continued to speak to the ghosts or to heaven or clouds, or whatever it was she was talking to.

'Do you hear me up there? Look, I'm going into the kitchen and pouring myself a glass of milk. See? I'm forty-six years old and I've sold all your things and I'm walking around your house as naked as a jaybird.' She looked around the room again and remembered how Carrie always locked everything up so tight, afraid of being broken into, afraid of rapists, robbers. Just afraid. 'I'm going to leave the window open tonight, Mama. If robbers break in through the window there'll be nothing to steal because it's all gone. It's all gone, Mama. I'm sorry, but I had to do it.' She was talking like a child who'd been scolded, like a forty-six-year-old child who'd done wrong. 'I just had to, Mama. Don't you see, there was nothing else I could do. All your little life is gone. Just . . . gone. I threw it out in black plastic bags. Thirty black plastic bags, Mama.'

She walked around the house again, then came back into the den. 'Mexicans bought your clothes, Mama. Black people bought your bedspreads. They walked across your carpets and touched your things.' She suddenly felt mean. She felt mean and sick. 'Somebody else is going to live here soon. They might even be white trash. Who knows, they may even cut down the dogwood tree. But there was nothing else I could do, Mama. It's all I could do.'

She sat on the edge of the mattress a long time, then went into the bathroom to put on her gown.

The karaoke at
Carrizozo Springs

The fifth of Willa Cather's kittens was born at the very
moment two tall, rather good-looking male strangers
knocked at the front door.

'Oh, dog do!' Perry hissed, then turned to Francis. 'Go see
who it is, will you? Whatever they want, you'll have to take care
of it. Our Cat simply can't bear to have me out of her sight right
now. She's absolutely traumatized, poor thing.'

Francis sighed and stood up from his seat, a needlepoint-
covered piano bench that had been rescued from old lady
Bradford's place just before her two brain-dead sons had
whisked her away to a 'home' in Roswell and sold all the rest of
her belongings to a junk dealer from Albuquerque. He went
over to the little window at the right of the front door and
peeked through the antique french-lace curtain.

'Well, well,' he said, partially to Perry and partially to
himself.

'Oh, for chrissakes, you know I hate it when you say "Well,
well,"' Perry barked at Francis. 'It's always just a blatant lure to
get me curious.'

Francis fluttered with excitement as he stepped back slightly
from the window. 'Well, all I can say is, one never knows when
one wakes up in the morning what little surprises one's gods
may have in store for one. Mmm. They're very pretty, Perry.
Come over here and take a look.'

'Oh, for god's sake! You know I can't move anywhere. Cat's in shock, poor thing. You know she's counting on me.'

Francis ran over to the bar, underneath which he had stashed his hairbrush, quickly ran it through his thinning hair and, darting a quick glance at himself in the bevelled etched mirror at the back of the bar – circa 1897, Vale, Colorado – he mustered as much composure as he could manage and went over to open the door. He put the safety chain on and unlatched the two locks, then stuck his nose through the crack.

'Can I help you?' he asked, friendly enough but with an air of caution. One of the strangers came forward and poked his head towards the open crack.

'Uh, well, sorry to bother you but we noticed your sign and . . .' He gestured above him at the old sign with peeling paint hanging at the top of the building which said 'Prine Brothers Mercantile'. 'We were just wondering if you were open or . . .'

'There's another one coming!' Perry yelled from inside. 'Lord, the poor thing must be absolutely *drained*.'

The man at the door glanced back at his friend.

'I'm sorry,' Francis said, peeking through the crack as he noticed the strangers exchanging looks of wariness, 'Our Willa Cather is having babies. It's her first litter so we're rather – paternal, I guess you'd say. You know how it is. Were you looking for anything in particular?'

'Oh, well, no,' the man outside replied, again turning to his friend. The other man stepped up beside him.

'We were just driving through, actually, on our way down to Mexico, and your place looked so interesting that . . .'

The door suddenly shut, the strangers could hear the chain being taken off and then it opened wide.

'You have an English accent! Perry, it's an Englishman! We haven't heard the King's English spoken around here since another man, Simon I think his name was, stopped by two years ago. Of course there's Masterpiece Theatre on NET and those wildlife documentaries you get with David Attenborough every now and then but, my, my, do come in!' The two men sheepishly grinned at each other and stepped inside.

The Prine Brothers Mercantile, originally named 'Prine's Mercantile' in 1891 when Perry and Francis' great-uncle Stephen Prine established it, had undergone various incarnations over the hundred-odd years of its existence. What had started out to be a general store, providing dry goods and basic supplies for the ranchers and miners in the area, had been turned into a bar when the brothers' father, George, had taken it over in the 1930s. When George died in the mid-sixties neither Perry, who was living in New York at the time, nor Francis, who was living in San Francisco, could bring themselves to move back to New Mexico. But they couldn't bring themselves to part with the property either. Every year they would meet at the Albuquerque airport, rent a van and start touring the state and the fringes of the surrounding states, stopping at little out of the way trading posts, little junk shops in the middle of nowhere, garage sales, estate sales, buying whatever struck their fancy. Sometimes it was an iron bedstead or a carved Mexican latillia. Other times there were pieces of wicker furniture, old wagon wheels, butter churns, Indian jewelry, old Navajo rugs, an etched glass aquarium, storm lanterns, Victorian lace nightgowns, old straw hats. They would then drive down to Carrizozo Springs and stash their new-found possessions in the store, barely taking time to arrange things in any order. They would reset the mousetraps, make sure the roof didn't leak and attend to any other minor problems that had sprung up in their year's absence. Then they'd return to Albuquerque, bid each other adios and go back to their lives in the cities.

'I think she's finally finished,' Perry said, looking over his shoulder at the two strangers. Another cat, a ginger tom, perched on the counter of the heavily carved wooden bar. 'It's all your fault, D.H., and you can't talk your way out of this one. Half the kittens are ginger, just like you.' Yet another cat, a large black and white one with white boots for feet jumped up from behind and onto the upright piano which was positioned at one side of the bar. It walked across the keys as though on a mission to get attention. 'Oh, Frieda, don't be jealous. I'm sure it was just a one-night stand.' Perry ran his hand across Frieda's back.

'I'm Perry, by the way.' Perry stretched out the same hand to shake hands with the strangers. 'And this is my brother, Francis.' All the men shook hands.

'I'm Ian and this is Ben,' said the man whose English accent was the softer of the two.

'Oh, Ian's such a British name, isn't it,' Francis swooned.

'Well, Ben certainly isn't,' Perry said. 'It's the name of one of those horrible Cartwright brothers in "Bonanza". But we'll forgive you,' he chuckled.

Ben managed a smile. This was his first trip to America. He'd started out in Vancouver, taken a Greyhound down to San Francisco, another to L.A., yet another to the Grand Canyon where he'd camped out for two days, then, finally, a last bus to Albuquerque. Ian, an old family friend who'd emigrated from England to New Mexico twelve years before, had picked him up at the bus station in 98 degree temperatures and whisked him away to his house in the north valley. Over the few days that followed, Ian had shown Ben around and now they were headed for Mexico. In the time they'd spent together Ben had come to realize that he and Ian had little in common – he'd never known him that well before – but Ian was someone to travel with and he knew the ins and outs of how to get around, so Ben was grateful to him regardless of their personality differences.

'This is quite a place you have here,' Ian said, walking around, inspecting things. Ben followed his lead and began to move around the room too.

'Yes, well, we like to think it's home,' Perry said. He followed behind and noticed Ian's interest in the old clock. 'It really works,' he said. He reached under the clock and retrieved a key to wind it. 'We just don't bother to keep it wound most of the time. It has a chime on the hour that sorta disturbs Sylvia.' Perry looked around and spotted the gray cat hiding under the fern stand at the side of the piano. He reached over, picked her up and began stroking her. 'Sylvia's rather intense, I'm afraid. She's been like that since she was little. It's because she almost got gassed. Which is how she got her name, of course. You see, her mother was in the process of moving all her kittens to a new place one day and somehow the oven door in the kitchen had been left open so she decided this was the perfect place to move them. Well, she'd moved Sylvia and had gone back to get one of the others when Francis came into the kitchen to heat up a casserole dish from the night before. He put the dish in the oven without seeing Sylvia and closed the door. He turned the oven on and was just about to push the lighter button – you know, one of those fire-starter things they have on some stoves – when Sylvia's mother came back with another kitten in her mouth. She dropped the kitten and started desperately pawing at the oven. Luckily Francis was alert enough to turn off the oven and he finally discovered the poor little thing. But we think it did permanent psychological damage.'

Ian and Ben stretched out on separate double beds in their room at the Rest-a-While motel. Perry and Francis had given them directions on how to get to the motel when it was decided that it was too late in the day for the two travellers to venture into Mexico. As it had turned out, Perry and Francis had led Ian and Ben through an extensive excursion down memory lane for hours. As they told it, after years of accumulating objects and stashing them in the store, the two brothers met during the summer of '75 and decided they'd each, in their separate ways, reached a turning point in their lives. New York and San Francisco were growing increasingly hectic and expensive and

Perry had just broken up with a long-time lover. Francis had yet to meet his dream-man and had thought that perhaps what he needed was a refocusing of his life in other directions. So, the two decided to return to Carrizozo Springs and take a stab at reopening the mercantile as an antique shop. As they'd described how they'd come to find each object in the store, related the mercantile's history to them, served them lunch – omelettes and refried beans – and even brewed them a perfect pot of tea, the first decent tea Ben had tasted since leaving England, Ben had found himself warming to the two men. When he and Ian had tried to leave at three, they'd encountered a barrage of protests from Perry and Francis who'd insisted they stay for dinner and the 'evening's events'. Not being able to imagine what such events might be, they had managed as politely as possible to decline the offer and they were just about to leave when they heard the shuffle of feet on the front porch and loud knocking. Perry and Francis froze, stern looks replacing the friendly warmth of moments before.

'Perriwinkle and Franciscan monk fucked each other until they stunk,' three loud male voices chanted from outside. There was wild laughter and more knocking at the door.

'Fancy Francey, fairy Perry.' Again, more laughter. Someone kicked something on the front porch.

Perry straightened himself up and calmly walked behind the bar. He pulled out his twenty-two, wiped the barrel off with a bar towel and walked over to the door. Francis scurried out to the kitchen. Ben noticed Francis was nervously humming 'Oh What a Beautiful Morning' to himself as he shut the door to the kitchen behind him.

Perry stood at the front door.

'What do you want?' he yelled at the men on the front porch who were really teenage boys. Raucous laughter could be heard.

'I said, what do you want?'

'Prine, swine, sweetheart of mine, fuck you in the ass until you whine.' With that the laughter grew even more hysterical.

'If you have no reason to be here then I suggest ...' At that moment a large brick crashed through the front picture window shattering glass that fell on all the surrounding objects inside. Two of the cats leapt behind the bar. Before Ben and Ian knew what was happening Perry had opened the door wide and was standing there, his gun raised and aimed at the offending youths.

'Get out of here, you trash. I'll give you to three. One ...' The boys continued laughing but stepped back from the store, further out into the street. 'Two ...' The boys stopped laughing and took a few more steps back. 'Three.' Perry fired at the feet of the three boys who scattered. He fired again and then fired a third time. The boys raced away. Perry stepped outside onto the porch. Ben and Ian, pale-faced, casting disbelieving looks at each other, shyly followed behind him. They saw the teenage boys running down the street. The three other buildings on the street, a post office, a greasy-spoon called Dot's Café and a garage, appeared empty. It was a veritable ghost town, one Ben and Ian had taken little notice of when they'd driven in. Aside from the boys running away in the distance, nobody else could be seen. Perry sighed and shook his head. He turned and went back into the store.

'All clear,' he yelled to Francis in the kitchen. He took a broom out from behind the bar, walked over to the window and began sweeping up the broken glass. Francis came out of the kitchen and propped the door open.

'I'm sorry, but could one of you gentlemen please be of service for a moment?' Ben looked at Ian and they moved towards Francis. When they came into the kitchen they saw Francis dusting off a large piece of plate glass.

'If one of you could be so kind as to just take one end of this we can get this mess over with as quickly as possible.' Ben lifted one side of the heavy glass as Francis lifted the other and they made their way out of the kitchen and towards the broken window.

'Maybe you could bring that little kit,' Francis said to Ian, nodding in the direction of a tool-box which sat on the kitchen counter. Ian, tool-box in hand, followed the others over to the front window. Perry was already breaking away the rest of the glass from the edges of the window. In a matter of minutes the two men were cleaning out the grooves of the window encasement and preparing it for mounting the new piece of glass.

Ben and Ian stood and watched as the two brothers expertly went about the business of installing the new window glass.

'Looks like you've done this before,' Ian said incredulously.

'Oh, you could say that,' Perry answered without looking up.

'If you cared to look you'd see six panes of glass just this same size in the pantry just off the kitchen,' Francis said as he concentrated on holding the glass in position as Perry did the carpentry. 'It should last us three or four months, hopefully.'

'You mean this happens ... often?' Ben asked, finding the whole experience more bizarre as the moments passed.

'Every two or three weeks,' Perry answered nonchalantly. 'It's this little game we have to play with the locals. They let their kids come here and call us names and cause trouble and throw bricks at our windows and, in exchange,' he grunted as he pushed the edge of the window in place, 'we don't get railroaded out of town, tarred and feathered.' Perry stopped what he was doing for a moment and looked at the two men.

'It's the real big bad west, isn't it,' he winked at them and smiled to himself as he wiped his hands on his jeans. 'I tell you what. If you really want to experience the real west come back tonight.' Perry looked over at Francis and grinned.

'Well, it won't exactly be Clint Eastwood,' Francis added to Perry's invitation, 'but, did you ever see "Destry Rides Again" with Marlene Dietrich? Anyway, you must come. We'll be simply distraught if you say no.'

So, eventually Ian and Ben had promised to return and had found their way to the Rest-a-While Motel, checked in, and now they lay on their beds thinking all sorts of things, the chief one being that maybe they were crazy. Crazy for even considering going back to such weirdness. Thinking they should probably just get a few hours' sleep, then check out and head towards the border.

Neither could explain to the other why or how it was that two hours later they were getting out of the car once again and walking up the stairs of the front porch of the Prine Brothers Mercantile. To make it worse, the sun winked at them as it dipped behind the chamisa on the west mesa.

Perry answered the door this time. He looked out the little window first, then, seeing Ben and Ian, quickly opened up. D.H. seized the opportunity and ran out between Ben's legs as the two men entered.

'Behave yourself, D.H.,' Perry yelled after him. 'We don't want you messing around with the wrong kind. Cats look pretty funny tarred and feathered.' The cat sat in the middle of the road, swishing his tail behind him, staring back up at the men as though considering what he'd just been told.

Just as Perry was about to close the door another vehicle drew up to the curb. It was a two-ton GMC pick-up with a camper shell. A man and a woman got out and waved at Perry, then went around to the back of the truck and opened the camper. A couple of minutes later they were hauling equipment into the store.

'Ralph, you shaved your beard!' Perry said, taking one of the speakers out of Ralph's arms. Ralph put the other speaker down in front of the bar. He shyly turned towards the two strangers and Perry introduced them. 'Ralph's our equivalent of a roadie,' Perry explained as he observed Ben and Ian curiously watching as Ralph began to set up the sound system and karaoke machine around the bar area. 'And this is Madeline. She is, how shall we say it, the mother of Ralph's children.'

'What he means to say is I live with Ralph and we have two

kids and we're not married which, around here, is excuse
enough to railroad *us* out of town too.' She gave Ben and Ian a
huge wider-than-Texas kind of smile and shook their hands like
a truck driver. Ralph nodded at them and kept himself busy
rigging up the sound equipment. At that moment Francis came
buzzing out of the kitchen. He had a baker's apron on over a
white tuxedo shirt with ruffles. He was barefoot.

'Ralph! Look at your face. It's so white!' Ralph mumbled
something in reply. 'Well, I suppose this must mean you're
trying to find a new image for yourself. After all, lumberjacks
are cute and everything but they must get tired of all that fuzzy
stuff all over their faces after a while.' Madeline laughed a raw,
belly-aching laugh.

'He's about as ready to get a new image as I'm ready to be the
president's wife,' she said, hitting Ralph on the back and almost
making him lose his balance. 'It happened because I started
trimming it for him the other day and the phone rang and it was
Jeanette over in Silver Springs and you know how we can talk
once we get going, and by the time I finally got off the phone and
walked into the bedroom, Ralph had been trying to even up the
beard on the other side I hadn't cut yet. Then he cut that side too
short, so he tried to even it up on the other side again and on and
on till the whole beard got down to just the stubs and he looked
sorta like Don whats-his-name on "Miami Vice". When I told
him that, he was so disgusted he said shit and went into the
bathroom and shaved the whole thing off.'

Everyone laughed and then their attention was drawn to the
sound of another car door closing. Madeline and Francis walked
over to the door, Ben following behind, as Ian hung around the
area where Perry and Ralph were rigging up the sound
equipment.

'It's Maude!' Madeline said and ran down the steps of the
porch to greet her. Maude was already pulling an ice chest out of
the back of her '69 vw stationwagon by the time Madeline
arrived at her side to help her. Ben followed.

'Ben, this is Maude. Maude, Ben,' Madeline introduced the two. Ben reached his hand out, then pulled it back when he saw that Maude had picked up the heavy ice chest all on her own and was already heading towards the porch.

'Nice meetin' ya,' she said. 'Scuse me if I don't shake. This thing's got enough cerveza in it to float the goddamn Mexican navy. Come to think of it, they even got such a thing as a Mexican navy?' she asked Francis on her way into the store. Madeline handed Ben a brown paper bag full of plastic cups and paper plates and jars full of potato salad and pickles. She picked up another bag from the back of the vw and they started carrying them into the store. As they got to the porch another car pulled up to the curb.

'Oh, it's Butch and Juan,' she said, managing to wave at the two men who were getting out of the white Toyota. 'Wonder where David is? Hi, guys. Where's David?'

'Oh, he'll be here in a minute. He got all caught up in decorating his devilled eggs,' the tall, well-built black man named Butch answered.

Ben couldn't help staring as Juan came around the car and into his view. Juan's long black hair was drawn back into a ponytail and he wore a pair of women's fifties rhinestone-trimmed sunglasses. His tight white shorts and Hawaiian shirt with hula dancers on it were accented by the score of paper-flowered leis around his neck, and on his feet were a pair of black patent elevated ankle boots. Maude whistled at him from the doorway.

'Juan, you get more like your uncle José as the days go by,' she hooted in reference to Juan's attire. Juan ran up to her on the porch and took off one of the leis and put it around Maude's neck.

'Mui bueno, darling,' he said as he kissed her on her cheek and headed inside the store.

The group went about getting organized. Madeline, Francis and Maude martialled Ben into helping them put the food out on a large hand-carved Mexican table that had been cleared for the evening. Perry, Butch, Ralph and Ian began clearing an open space in front of the bar and setting up a row of chairs. Juan busied himself with stringing a set of tiny Christmas lights around the bar and plugging them in. They twinkled on and off. Another car could be heard pulling up and Madeline stuck her head out the door to see who it was. Then another one came behind, the driver shouted something and Madeline went outside. Ralph turned on the stereo, Mexican salsa music filled the air and the first of the Mexican beers was uncapped. The cats had already retreated to their favorite hiding places.

Larry entered with a big bottle of bourbon wrapped in a brown paper bag. He took off his stetson and greeted everyone heartily as Claire, his wife, added a piping hot pot of barbecue beans to the table of food. David came behind them with his devilled eggs and was greeted by Francis, Butch and Juan. Maude went over to Ben who she could see was standing off at the side of the group, watching everything with total absorption. Ian seemed to be deeply entrenched in a conversation with Ralph and Butch.

'Quite a bunch, huh?' she said as she gave Ben a Dos Equis.

'Quite,' he answered, smiling sweetly at her. He hadn't really seen her close up until now. One of her eyes was rather cloudy as though she had cataracts or glaucoma – he couldn't remember which it was that caused an eye to look that way – and her face was like soft leather, maybe like deer skin, although he couldn't really say he was that familiar with what deer skin looked like either. She was little – came up to his shoulder – and wiry, but she had a toughness about her that showed itself in her posture and gestures. Her hands were quite large for such a small person and there seemed to be dirt under her short-cut fingernails. She held her hands together down in front of her and rocked on her heels when she stood in one place.

'Must seem pretty far-out to you I guess. I hear you're from London England.' She cast a quick look up at him then quickly darted her eyes back to the others. 'Never been to London England. Or Paris France either. Always wanted to though.'

'Really?'

'Aw, sure. After all, my folks come from around there somewhere. I mean, not my close relatives or anything, but you know what I mean, *originally*.' Ben smiled. He'd already gathered that almost everybody in America claimed some sort of ancestral connection with Britain.

'What're you doin' all the way over here?' Again, she darted a look at him, then averted her eyes. Ben explained he was on holiday and that he'd come to visit Ian who was an old family friend.

'Humph,' she grunted good-heartedly. 'Holiday, huh. I guess that's what we call a vacation over here. Wish I could take a vacation. Can't even seem to make it up to Grants these days. It's one thing after another, you know, with the station and all. Keeps you busy.'

'Station?' Ben was trying to figure out what she meant. Did she work at a railroad station somewhere or a bus station?

'Yeah. Oh, well a course. I forgot, how could you know? I run the Texaco over at Bottom Wash. Keeps me so busy I barely even got any time to go see my daughter up in Grants. She works at the prison up there. Teaches English. She even gets people to come in and do these special workshops with some of those prisoners. You know, these special writing workshops. Larry over there did one a couple a weeks ago. That reminds me.' Maude turned towards Larry who was talking to Madeline and Perry. 'Hey, Larry, how'd that workshop up in Grants go? Larry's a poet, you see,' she turned back to Ben to explain.

'Poet!' Ben almost exclaimed out loud but managed to keep it to himself. So far there was an old lady who ran a gas station in a place called Bottom Wash, a cowboy poet and his wife, Ralph, who seemed to be some kind of lumberjack, and his partner, Madeline, and Perry and Francis, whose occupations Ben could not quite put a label on. God only knew what Butch, David and

Juan did. Larry moved over to Maude and they started talking
about the workshop he'd conducted at the prison in Grants.
When Ben asked how he managed to survive being a poet living
in such a remote place Larry laughed.

'Well, you see, I inherited my father's ranch about ten years
ago. That's really what I *do*. What I *am* is a poet.' Claire joined
them. She'd heard Ben's English accent and was full of
questions about Yorkshire which, as she began filling in Ben in
detail, was where she had been born and lived until her
American father had left her English mother and moved back to
the U.S. when she was seven.

It was after dark when the black Ford pulled in at the side of
the store and Perry and Francis tore themselves away from the
group and went outside to meet the late arrivals. Ben and Maude
walked over to the door too. Ben had still not shaken off the
trauma of earlier in the afternoon, and although Perry and
Francis didn't appear in the least bit nervous about the
seemingly hostile community that resided somewhere near, Ben
couldn't quite bring himself to relax. He saw two men and a
woman getting out of the black car, a dusty old model that
looked like it could have come from the fifties. The woman got
out of the back seat and seemed to be trying to help an older man
get out of the passenger's side of the car. A younger man got out
on the driver's side. The old man had some kind of wooden
container in his arms and the lady carried a large brown bag.
The group slowly made their way to the porch where Ben was
introduced.

Roy looked at least a hundred years old to Ben's eyes. But
given the natural elements in this part of the world, Ben guessed
he was probably in his eighties. He walked curled over, his spine
bent from too many years of hard work Ben guessed, and he had
a scraggly gray beard and wore an old felt hat. Red braces,
suspenders they called them here, held up his blue jeans, at the
bottom of which stood a pair of very worn cowboy boots. The
woman, Sandy she was called, was his daughter. Ben had heard a

lot of 'quaint' expressions on his trip so far and one of them immediately came to mind in reference to Sandy: she was as plain as a fence post. But when she opened her mouth to speak her appearance became animated, full of infectious energy and it was as though a curtain lifted from her mousy brown eyes to reveal an altogether different person.

Joe, on the other hand, had given Ben little time to size him up. He'd briefly spoken hello to him, then headed straight into the store. His appearance was unexceptional except for his rather greasy longish hair and unkempt clothes. Ben watched as the three were heartily received by the group. Perry found what seemed to be a seat of honor for Roy to sit in and Madeline brought him a plate filled with food from the table. Sandy busily chatted to Claire and Larry as she filled her plate. Ben then realized the reason for Joe's hasty retreat into the store. Juan was brushing back Joe's hair, placing a lei around his neck and speaking in low affectionate tones to him. As the group shifted, David and Butch became engrossed in conversation with Maude and Francis. Ian sat on the piano bench, charming the pants off of Madeline and Sandy. Perry came over to Ben.

'Well, what do you think?' he said as he stared out across his assembled friends. 'Never would've guessed such an amazing and diverse bunch of people could be living in such a desolate and forbidding place as this, would you?' Ben smiled and shook his head but was at a loss as to what to reply.

'It's a long story, of course,' Perry continued, 'how we all found each other. But then it always is I guess.' Ben felt himself relax with that thought. He suddenly wondered if all these people had 'found each other' the same way he and Ian had found Perry and Francis.

'But anyway, I think it's time we got on with the show. Ralph . . .' Perry moved towards the bar and Ralph came over to help him. Ben saw them plug in and place a small hand microphone on the bar countertop. Ralph turned a couple of knobs on the equipment and Perry started saying things like 'testing testing.'

193

Everybody took this as a cue and began taking their plates and drinks over to the seats. Juan headed to the back of the bar and turned on an overhead light that had been positioned to act as a spotlight on an area directly in front of the bar. He then went to the front door, closed and locked it, and turned out the other lights in the store. Ralph pushed a button on the system's panel and started a tape. A drum roll began, the group grew quiet and Francis stepped into the makeshift spotlight.

His baker's apron had been replaced by a black tuxedo and he'd painted bright pink harlequin spots on each cheek.

'Mesdames et messieurs, je suis enchanté, I mean I am ever so exceedingly pleased, in fact I'm abundantly *thrilled* to have all of you here once again for our live-and-in-full-color "At-the-End - of - a - Dusty - Road - in - the - Middle - of - Nowhere - with - a - Capital-N-Fifth-Annual-God-Knows-We-Do-Try   Celebration of Life-as-We-Know-It" in the year of our Lord 1992, at the Prine Brothers Mercantile of Carrizozo Springs, New Mexico, U.S.A., the World, the Cosmos and whatever else comes after that.' Everyone chuckled and cuddled up closer to one another.

'Well, it's been another exciting year here in our charming little community. Just to refresh all our memories, we have this year managed to survive the pollution from the forest fires up in the Gila Wilderness, the inconvenience of the road to Silver Springs being washed out in the spring floods, and other equally awe-inspiring events culminating in the major pile-up on Interstate 10 in May which resulted in traffic being re-routed through our town, bringing in new customers to delight and enrichen us for almost twenty-four hours.' Ben watched the old friends exchange quick knowing expressions as they continued to laugh at Francis' monologue.

'But, we are gathered here not out of nostalgia, although, god knows, it would be so easy to get caught up in our fond reminiscences of so many action-packed days full of the veritable panoply of stimulating and enlightening life-lived-at-the-cutting-edge experiences we've all crammed into our busy date books. No, we're also here to wash ourselves in the sparkling aura of the artistry that abounds from the very pores of those closest among us. So without further ado, I want you to put those hard-worked palms together and be extraordinarily kind and welcome our very own "Citrus Sisters". (They're just three fruits who want to have a good time.)'

Everyone applauded loudly as Francis stepped out of the spotlight and Ralph pushed another button. The taped musical introduction began as Juan, David and Butch rustled out from the kitchen over to the center of the spotlight. Each wore a headdress made up of grapefruits, limes and oranges and they were draped in one wide piece of chartreuse gauze.

'Oui, nous avons pas de bananes, nous avons pas de bananes aujourd'hui,' they began singing. They stood close to each other with their left shoulders turned towards the audience. Each time they got to the place in the song where they repeated 'oui, nous avons pas de bananes', they turned the opposite direction in unison.

'We've got prickly pears and cumquats and chillis and god-knows-whats but, oui nous avons pas de bananes, nous avons pas de bananes aujourd'hui.' The group loudly applauded, Ralph did his lumberjack whistle and, to Ben's amusement, he saw Ian shouting 'Encore, encore' from his place in the front row.

Encouraged by the reception they received, the trio ripped off the chartreuse gauze revealing themselves to be clad in skintight satin shorts and nothing else. Juan wore red, David black, and Butch white. They assumed three muscle-men poses as Ralph pushed the button again and the music began to play 'Y.M.C.A.'. The three began by belting out the words to the song, then they started moving out into and around the people in the audience, flirting outrageously with the men, winking at the women. Everyone died laughing then David spotted Ben. As they continued to sing he went over to Ben and started rolling his shoulder up against Ben's chest. Then Juan followed his lead and came over too and, pretending to vie with David for Ben's affection, began to run his fingers through Ben's hair. Finally, Butch joined the other two and, asserting his larger size, pretended to shove the other two men away. Before Ben knew what was happening, Butch lifted him and the three carried him to the spotlight. They finished their song by each wrapping various arms and legs around Ben. The roar of laughter from the group and the good-natured, un-threatening feeling from the trio over-rode Ben's embarrassment and by the end of the act he felt he'd been zapped to another planet. He was still soaring a few minutes later when Maude handed him another Dos Equis as the three men settled him down in a seat, smiled and patted him on the back.

'Guess the Brits must be pretty good sports,' Maude said and Ben was jolted into yet another surreal thought: he was being seen as an ambassador, a representative of his country. He tried to imagine how many other Brits would have taken this turn of events as acceptingly as he had.

'And now, my wonderful bouquet of wild flowers,' Francis continued in his role as Master of Ceremonies. 'In the spirit of exploiting the vast and multi-faceted talents of those in our midst, and in tune with our trio's first number, we shall proceed in the literary vein. For those of you who didn't already know, the stirring rendition of "Yes, We Have No Bananas" which our dear Citrus Sisters so winningly gave us, was originally translated into the French and used in a play by the poet e.e. cummings. So, in light of this, we continue to cultivate and entertain you with our very own local poet, Larry Wilcox.'

Everyone applauded enthusiastically and Larry stood up and walked into the spotlight.

'Well, I feel honored by following such a polished and literary act such as we've just happily witnessed. It's a hard act to follow, but I'll try to keep you from snoring too loudly with something I hope you can all relate to.' Larry cleared his throat and took a deep breath. Then he motioned to Ralph who pushed another button on the machine. The overture to Copland's 'Grand Canyon Suite' came on low and soft in the background. After a few moments, Larry stood up straight and stepped directly into the spotlight. He took a deep breath and looked straight at the audience as he began to recite.

> Snake trails, sea shells,
> residing in the undergrowth
> of where the ancient glacier moved,
> melting into dust.
>
> Trails and shells and tire-tracks
> and wagon ruts in the under-cut
> of life we've left behind
> in the desert where we desert
> the wrinkled maps of where we once
> thought we were going.
>
> I got my chaps on.
> I got chapped lips.
> I got a chapped ass
> because I went outside
> without my pants
> and the air was dry
> and the stars sang louder than usual
> and I had to sit down and listen.
>
> And as I sat on the mesa,
> things stirred in their night music.
> I kept my voice inside me.
> I wanted to call a coyote.
> I wanted a bear.
> I wanted to change into
> the shadow of the Palos Verde
> and dance like a witch.

And it got louder, this music.
It kicked at the echoes.
It raised a ruckus in the arroyo.
It howled at the puckered moon.

They have a name for it –
this sound life makes when
it's eaten well and slept good
and done strong things all day long.
It's called conga
like a heart drum
like thick blood, sangre,

like knowing you are on
the trail to ever after
and it goes nowhere and returns
on the other side.

The music crescendoed and Ralph stepped back from the spotlight. Whatever it meant, Ben felt himself moved. He wasn't one for poetry and, as he looked around, he realized that probably no one else in the room was either. He had no way of knowing whether or not the poem was any good but somehow it didn't matter because, as the friends in the room all clapped, their faces showed true love for Larry's language, for its reference to the things they knew and somehow all understood, for the common feeling they all seemed to have for one another.

Francis came back to the spotlight after the applause had settled down.

'Well, good people, I think you will agree we are indeed fortunate to be blessed by such a reminder of our little place in the cosmos and we can each retire later with a sense of having been uplifted and transported to a world that none of us usually frequents on a day to day basis, except, perhaps, for Larry here. But even Larry, I'm sure, doesn't always inhabit the other world of poetic communion when he's out there roundin' up them dogies and wondering if it's chow time yet. Ah, home on the ol' prairie. And, although those stars out there are now mingled with space ships from other galaxies and satellites bringing us the very best in pornography from Denmark, we can take small comfort from those who still hold dear some of the traditions of our past. And so, on that note, I'd like to introduce to you our next act. It's one we are proud to bring back to you by popular demand, one that lifted our hearts mightily last year when it was performed for the first time. Ladies and Gents, I'm proud to present our Miss Sandy and Roy!'

Loud whistles and yelling abounded as the old man and his daughter rose and headed towards the spotlight. Juan placed a chair in the centre of the 'stage' and Roy sat down. Sandy pulled a saw out of the brown paper bag she'd had sitting by her side and handed it to Roy. Roy took the red bandanna from around his neck and wrapped it around his right hand, then positioned the saw between his knees as he pulled out a bow from the bag. Sandy went over to the out-of-tune piano and played a few chords, then she cut into the musical introduction as Ralph started the machine again, this time the sounds being those of a drum playing in waltz-time.

> Good night, Irene, Irene,
> Good night, Irene.
> Good night, Irene, good night, Irene,
> I'll see you in my dreams.

Roy's voice was hoarse and craggy but it still had an amazing strength to it as he began the first verse. He expertly maneuvered the saw which produced strange tinny but rather steel-guitar-like sounds. Sandy sang in harmony with him during the choruses. After the first two verses, the rest of the group began to chime in. By the end of the song, Roy put the saw down, Ralph faded out the drum sounds and the group sang, in harmony and in a cappella, the chorus they all knew and loved. Even Ben knew it, it was almost as familiar to him as it was to the rest of the group, and he found himself swaying right to left with the row of people he sat amongst. Ian was swaying too. They caught each other's eye during the fourth and final repeat of the chorus and smiled. Ian was as astonished and overwhelmed by the whole thing as Ben was.

Again, everybody applauded loudly and whistled. At this point, Perry joined Francis and together they stepped into the spotlight.

'Well, although Roy and Sandy's act is virtually impossible to follow, unfortunately we've come to the place in the show where it's time for Perry and yours truly, the hosts and benevolent masters of this establishment, to put in our two cents' worth. So, we'd like to perform for you tonight a little ditty from the fifties, made famous by those poor unliberated virgins of yesteryear, Patience and Prudence, in their bid for immortality. Patience and Prudence, wherever you are, even if it's a trailer home park in Norman, Oklahoma, you remain immortal in these old queens' hearts to this day.' With that, Ralph pushed another button and music began once again.

> Have faith, hope and charity,
> that's the way to live successfully.
> How do I know? The Bible tells me so.
>
> Be good to all your enemies
> and the good Lord you are sure to please.
> How do I know? The Bible tells me so.
>
> Don't worry 'bout tomorrow, just be real good today.
> The Lord is sure to find you and take you on his way.
>
> Have faith, hope and charity,
> that's the way to live successfully.
> How do I know? The Bible tells me so.

After the first run through, Juan, Butch and David returned to join Perry and Francis on the stage. Across the chest of each man was a white satin ribbon like one a beauty queen might wear. Juan's ribbon had the word 'Faith' sewn on it in red sequins, Butch, 'Hope' and David, 'Charity'. Hands on hips, they positioned themselves around Francis and Perry as each of the brothers cuddled up to them. They sang in perfect harmony. Once again, by the time the song came to an end, the whole group was singing along with the performers.

The homemade peach ice-cream Roy had churned in his ice-cream maker after the show ended was topped with crushed pecans Maude had shelled. Out in the kitchen corks could be heard popping and Perry brought out two bottles of California champagne as Francis followed with a silver tray of Italian crystal champagne glasses. One round of toasts followed another, two more bottles were uncorked and before he knew it, Ben was following the others out of the store and into the night. Even a little drunk, he couldn't completely abandon the idea that they were leaving the store empty and wide-open, easy prey for whatever elements in the area might want to take advantage of the situation. But he reminded himself that these people probably knew what they were doing and so he kept his mouth shut and followed along. Somewhere along the way he found himself walking next to Ian. They started to speak to each other, but when they caught each other's eye they simply laughed. It was a laugh of understanding, of knowing words would never be enough. No matter how many times either would try to describe this night, they would never be able to completely relate the real experience. They knew that this was something they'd shared, and that, whatever else they did together, whatever future adventures, this would be the one that found them, at least momentarily, bonded.

The mesa wasn't very high, just high enough to see the twinkling lights of a few houses in the distance and the red warning light at the top of a radio antenna on a nearby hill. The group chatted amongst each other as they walked along but the conversations grew quieter and more intimate. Maude and Sandy were walking arm in arm and Ralph gently held Roy's arm as they made it up the side of the mesa. With a quick burst of energy, Claire and Madeline raced Butch and Juan and Joe up the side as Larry and David walked more slowly, having become entrenched in a discussion about the fossils each collected. As Ben surveyed the group he saw Perry and Francis strolling, arm in arm, like two southern belles holding parasols. It was dark so Ben couldn't actually see their faces, but he thought they walked as if contented, as though they were savoring each moment.

They all sat scattered out along the rim of the mesa. The air was fragrant with wild sage and chamisa. As if on cue, as if someone had said 'quiet!', they all drew silent. At first Ben's ears seemed to ring. It sounds like black snow, he thought. It was as though some internal space had been invaded, some chamber inside him opened up for the first time; he had never heard such nothingness. And the sky. There was no moon, no light, just an infinity of stars. Bags of the finest sugar spilled across the sky. Sweet stars.

Ben lay back on the soft mesa sand. Tomorrow Mexico. In a week, home. Tonight, here. At just this place. On the trail to ever after. And it goes nowhere. And returns.